Karen Hitchcock's fiction has ap...
Australian Stories 2006, 2007 and *2006, Families: Modern Australian Stories, Sunday Life, Meanjin, Griffith Review* and *The Sleepers Almanac*. She works as a doctor and is also a lecturer in Medicine at the University of Newcastle, where she has recently completed a PhD in English/ Creative Arts.

Little White Slips is her first collection of stories.

Little White Slips

PICADOR
Pan Macmillan Australia

First published 2009 in Picador by Pan Macmillan Australia Pty Limited
1 Market Street, Sydney

National Library of Australia
Cataloguing-in-Publication data:
Hitchcock, Karen.
Little White Slips / Karen Hitchcock.
ISBN 9780330424998 (pbk.)
A823.4

The characters and events in this book are fictitious and any resemblance
to real persons, living or dead, is purely coincidental.

Typeset in 12/15.5 pt Bembo by Midland Typesetters, Australia
Printed by McPherson's Printing Group

Papers used by Pan Macmillan Australia Pty Ltd are natural, recyclable
products made from wood grown in sustainable forests. The manufacturing
processes conform to the environmental regulations of the country of origin.

For Mowbray

We're all in this alone.

— *Lily Tomlin*

Contents

Drinking When We Are Not Thirsty

Q 1.

A 60-year-old male has a cardiac arrest in the community. Paramedics attend within 5 minutes and he is defibrillated unsuccessfully 3 times. Which drug, if administered next, would be most likely to result in a successful cardioversion in this setting?

(a) Bretylium

(b) Amiodarone

(c) Lignocaine

(d) Bicarbonate

(e) Magnesium

My husband Ed shrugs when I tell him about the specialist physician exams. 'I teach algebra to thirty screaming kids each day for Christ's sake, Jessica. I'm sure Katie and I can cope.' I want to tell him he knows shit about shit, but I bend down and give Katie a big squeeze. 'Mummy needs to study. A lot. A whole lot. But soon it'll all be over, and we'll go to the park and on a holiday and visit the chocolate factory and the museum and the zoo. Okay, honey?' She looks at my face then looks at the ground. I ask Ed if he should apply for long service leave and take Katie to stay with his mother. I tell him I'll be working all day and studying all night, that he'll have to do it all. He gives me that look. He thinks I'm being hysterical again.

So I start on the Monday night. Ed's in the car with Katie driving home from childcare and I'm separating the body into specialties: Cardiology, Gastroenterology, Endocrinology, Neurology. Immunology, Rheumatology, Haematology, Oncology. Respiratory, Infectious Diseases, Nephrology. I allocate three weeks to each system. I lug *Harrison's* to my desk where it will sit unopened for six months like an anachronistic, beautifully illustrated mascot. I make a cup of tea.

Q 2.

A 50-year-old female presents with a 3-month history of a distal, symmetrical polyarthritis. Her blood tests reveal the following:

Rheumatoid Factor: 45
Extractable Nuclear Antigen anti-Ro: Positive
Double stranded DNA: Negative
Anti-CCP: Negative
Ribosomal P-Protein: Positive
ANA titre: Speckled 1:160, N1:640

Which of the following is the most likely diagnosis?

(a)   Systemic lupus erythematosus
(b)   Rheumatoid arthritis
(c)   Mixed connective tissue disease
(d)   Systemic sclerosis
(e)   Primary Sjogren's syndrome

On Wednesday nights after work I attend core-curriculum lectures televised by the College of Physicians. The chairman is a cranky old general physician with an ashtray voice and a fatherly manner that veils his temper. *Hepcidin?* he says, *never heard of it . . . But it seems as if you have to know it inside out.* I have an instant crush on the man that activates each week as soon as he appears on-screen and is forgotten the moment I step out of the theatre into the dim hospital corridor. I spend the lecture hours composing admiring emails and imagining clandestine meetings where he pours that soft gravel into my ear and down my neck. *Sweetheart, you know those four types of renal tubular acidosis yet?* While Ed and Katie eat spaghetti and read bedtime stories, nine male registrars and I sit in the dark freeze of the Grand Rounds lecture theatre, scrawling notes, praying, perspiring.

On the weekends I fill a bowl with Sultana Bran and close my study door. Ed loads up the pram and takes Katie to places I can no longer even imagine: libraries, galleries, museums, the beach. I feel better when the house empties of their chatter and music and squeals, when the signs of life drain away, leaving me a void. On the weekends I do use *Harrison's*: the fat tome perfectly elevates my laptop to eye level, and this is the best level for viewing web-stream revision lectures, PowerPoint presentations and the iTunes store.

I have to stop working the overtime shifts that were paying our mortgage. I need the time to study. Ed nods tensely and says we can cope for six months on the MasterCard and the overdraft. I remind him of the future, when I'll work half-time and cover all the payments. When I'll have time to be a better mother, a better wife, a better person. He snorts, and I want to kill him. It is not long before all conversation between

Ed and me becomes bristle and snare. When I finally finish my training – this exam, then three more years – I'll be forty-five years old and Katie will be eight. I do the sums – my age plus the bank interest minus Katie's youth – and then flick them from my mind, like scabs.

Q 3.

A 65-year-old female residing in a developed country has an average life expectancy of how many more years?

(a) 5

(b) 10

(c) 15

(d) 20

(e) 30

In the hospital from eight till six, my mind overflows onto scraps of paper. I carry handfuls of scrawled-on, screwed-up paper. My resident asks me if she should repeat a patient's blood gas and I say, 'Mr Whose blood gas?', and shuffle my scraps. The consultant asks me how Mrs Thomas fared through the night and I say, 'Mrs Thomas, Mrs Thomas,' and shuffle my scraps. 'Mrs Thomas, that's right, she's in ICU after a respiratory arrest.' What's the result of the head CT, the electrolytes, the high-dose dexamethasone, the short-synacthen? What should we do? I dance my new dance: The Shuffle and Sweat. Some scraps have lists of things I don't know: statin guidelines, thrombolysis contra-indications, Sjogren's syndrome, sarcoidosis, Von Willebrand's disease. I throw nothing made of paper away. It could contain the name of a disease I need to learn, a disease that may turn up in the exam. I am bombarded with unknown words, like piercing, anxiety-provoking bullets; I have to spread my arms out wide to welcome them and I am full of holes.

I scoff when I look at my wardrobe floor – all those high-heels! I used to wear them to work. I used to wear lipstick and perfume and earrings. I used to spend *whole minutes* choosing earrings, holding them to my earlobes, ensuring they matched my outfit, looked stylish, wouldn't bang against my stethoscope. I had time for earrings. Now I wear khaki canvas jackets, with pockets – the more pockets the better – to catch the scraps shed from my brain.

Alone in my study week after week, I crave ridiculous, childish food: jelly-slice, Twisties, BBQ Shapes. The food of my childhood. I make a list. After the exam I can have all of this. I'll throw a party. I go to sleep dreaming about sinking my teeth into cold chocolate crackles, but during the day I live on tea and Sultana Bran. My study is a castle filled with fragile towers of paper – sharp and white – the sheer bulk of it sickening. A castle littered with cheap crockery, caked in yellow milk. I stare at the walls – slats of wood, just like a coffin. The word *fail* slaps against the ceiling like a trapped bat, and suddenly I am hot with panic. My daughter raps at the door.

'You studying, Mummy?'

I take my head out of my hands. 'Yes, sweetheart.'

I hear her lean against the door. 'You okay, Mummy?'

'Yes, sweetheart.' My head falls back into my hands.

She pushes her mouth against the hinge, her voice muffled. 'You need a cuddle?'

Q 4.

A young male presents with ACTH-dependent hyper-
aldosteronism. An MRI of his brain shows no abnormality.
What is the next most appropriate investigation?

(a)   High-dose dexamethasone suppression test

(b)   Petrosal sinus sampling

(c)   Octreotide scan

(d)   Corticotrophin-Releasing hormone level

(e)   Adrenal CT scan

A registrar named Troy – a recent arrival from Ireland –
asks me to study with him. He is tall and stick thin and
knows far more than me. We meet twice a week at a noisy
café in town to trawl through old exam papers. I apologise
for my ignorance. I tell him I'd understand if he joined
a different study group. He shakes his head and tells me
I'm being daft. 'I know,' I say. 'That's my point?' He sculls
ristretto after ristretto while I sip tea. I tell him his coffee
matches his hair: thick and black. He apologises that he has
no simile for my tea. 'But it's lovely,' he says in his Irish.

'Well, you can have some,' I say, holding out my cup.

'I meant your hair, not your bloody tea.'

I touch my unwashed waves and – like a paranoiac –
immediately worry about his motive. 'Right, oh, thanks.'
I look down at the page. 'I was just wondering, do you
understand how oestrogen influences the formation of
bone?' Of course he does.

I SMS him my questions a few times a day. I SMS
him like an adult, using correct spellings and full punctuation. He sculls, I sip and we wrestle one question

at a time, exchanging information, debating the facts, quoting review papers and lectures. We have to lean in close to hear each other's arguments. I hold out my scraps of paper like they're hard proof. He offers his memory piece by piece. Twice a week in that noisy café my anxiety sleeps and my skin is shocked alive by the bustle and knock of other people living. And by Troy's ristretto eyes.

The other nights I'm trapped in my study where the walls expand and deflate as if I'm in a big white lung. But if I'm in a lung, then why the hell can't I breathe? I need to get out, feel a breeze, take a walk, watch a movie. I need to see Troy. I SMS him a question about ACE-inhibitors, which he answers immediately, my reliable telephone encyclopaedia. But it's not enough. Maybe we could go for a walk, a study walk! I see Katie strapped into her car seat, limp-shouldered, staring at me standing at the front gate in my nightie, me smiling and waving goodbye like I'm psychotic. 'Bye, honey! Have fun! Do you need a spare dummy? See you tonight!' That little face staring. Child-deserters do not deserve walks.

Six weeks in, and neither Katie nor Ed will talk to me. Ed prickles when I look at him or touch him or try to help him. His shoulders and elbows, the profile of his jaw all tell me, *Stop fucking around, get back in your hole and work, you think I'm doing this for nothing?*

I ruminate about my brain's capacity for abuse; I thrash the poor thing with facts and reasons. I beat it up for not remembering. I thrash it and beat it and panic that it's broken.

I try to eat dinner with Ed and Katie but we roll through one script over and again:

> *Me, flicking through past exam papers:* This exam is so fucking hard.
> *Ed:* You want some more spaghetti, Katie?
> *Me:* I mean it is *so* hard. I don't see how I can possibly pass.
> *Ed:* Have you finished your milk, Katie?
> *Me:* I mean, what the hell is an anti-centromere antibody, anyway?
> *Ed: (feeds Katie spinach)*
> *Me:* What'd you do at childcare today, Katie?
> *Katie: (spits out spinach)*
> *Me:* How was work?
> *Ed: (mops up spinach)*

Saturday morning and Ed's standing at the door of my study, throwing threatening letters at me. 'Jessica, you have to deal with these.'

I relinquish a study day and fax my late registration to the NSW Medical Board, register as a trainee with the Royal Australian College of Physicians, register to sit the exam, pay for the revision weekend at Royal Prince Alfred, the College lecture series, and another revision weekend for next year, in case I fail. I renew my *UpToDate* online subscription and my medical registration in the UK. I can't afford my membership with the Australian Medical Association, I can't pay my medical indemnity.

I walk into the kitchen holding the electricity bill. 'What should we do about the electricity?' I ask him. 'There's nothing left in the account. And I still have to pay indemnity and the Australian Medical Association. Should I use the MasterCard again?' Ed has Katie cradled in his arms, her back to me. He points at my forehead, threatening my memory. 'If *we* can wait then fucking Energy Australia can wait, your indemnity can wait, and the Australian Medical Association can go and fuck themselves!'

It's not until late that night, lying in bed, that I wonder why I would pay for ongoing registration in the UK rather than for the electricity in my own house. I am vertiginous with guilt, but text Troy a question: *Do we give folic acid or folinic acid for MTX induced pancytopenia?* And right away, he gives me what I need: *Folinic acid. Sweet dreams.*

We have thirty-five dollars in the bank, the bills are flooding in, red and urgent, but to pause, to breathe, I shop online. The net is my street, my secret stroll. Face up close to the screen, searching, guiltily searching, for company or for something; shopping as if I'm fucking. Suddenly I desire decoration again. I buy shoes and hand-soaps, lingerie and stockings. Idly imagining his gaze one morning, I realise I am decorating myself for Troy. Betrayal though it is, I am unable to stop myself. I buy a heap of crap, hiding the packaging and the MasterCard statements from Ed.

I buy a tremendously expensive cactus necklace from Japan. It's a one-centimetre spiky plant in a glass vial on a nickel chain. I water it once a week, at my desk; immersing it in a shot glass of water, waiting for the vial to fill before draining it and gently setting the wet vial back on the windowsill, where it can catch the sun.

I buy boots from Topshop. I love that each pair only takes two days to arrive all the way from England. I pull them on and they have me teetering and towering around the bedroom Saturday mid-mornings; a drag queen in her pyjamas, with glasses, with her 'lovely' messed-up hair. I pose in front of the mirror then clip-clop back to my desk. Legs crossed, boots on show – red suede they are today – I abandon Haematology and move on to Immunology, an esoteric specialty where they experiment on flies bred without skin, where what's important are hundreds of microscopic enzymes, cytokines, little chemical bombs, with names coined in German laboratories, Chinese institutes, in the board-rooms of billion-dollar pharmaceutical companies. Most are a sequence of numbers and letters starting with 'C' or 'IL'. They are dull, indistinguishable and I need to know them all. I punch sticky notes onto the wall in front of me with my fist, engraving mad nomenclature into my corneas, wondering what the fuck I am doing. I text Troy: *When I was a teenager 'C3 and the Alternative Pathway' would've been a hardcore band, not a human defence system.* He replies: *Just know about C1-inhibitor deficiency and meet me for a coffee at 3.* It's one-fifteen. I read about C1-inhibitor deficiency, happily watching my boots, happily watching the time.

Q 5.

A 22-year-old male was rendered quadriplegic after a motor vehicle accident 12 weeks ago. He now has hypercalcemia. Measurement of his electrolytes reveal the following:

Ionised Calcium 1.8
Serum Calcium 3.1
Creatinine 150
Urea 6.4
PTH 30

What is the most likely cause of the hypercalcemia?

(a)   Vitamin D intoxication
(b)   Excess calcium intake from antacids
(c)   Rhabdomyolysis
(d)   Immobilisation
(e)   Primary hyperparathyroidism

My family is in tatters, but unbelievably Ed and I still fuck. Late into the night or early in the morning, we fuck efficiently, without kissing or words or eye contact. For the first time in my life I have sex with Ed and imagine he is someone else. My orgasms are quick and explosive and I fall asleep the moment I roll over. I wake up inside sweaty twisted sheets – wet and taut not from our non-wild love, but from fear and desire and my nightmares. I dream of Troy and of failure and death.

Katie runs in most mornings, jumps on the bed crying, 'Daddy, I had a bad dream,' or 'Daddy, I saw a fairy.' It's

Daddy this and Daddy that, while I lie on my wet side of the bed as if I'm in a sealed, empty bottle. They babble together happily and I float far, far away, caught up in some rip.

Ed and I no longer talk about the future. My career has become a despicable dictator, pointless to address. For us, there is only the hell of the present. At times I wonder if there is a part of Ed that likes this situation: his immaculate martyrdom, his limitless revenge. And what a pity I can't talk with my husband about the future, about the only thing that keeps me going. Very occasionally, when there is room for it, I imagine myself as a consultant Geriatrician, looking after all my old ladies with their soft-set white hair, and my old men with their plaid cotton handkerchiefs. Keeping them safe, treating their high blood pressures and pneumonias and coughs; treating their clots and their shaky old bones. Helping them live long and well. I describe this future to Troy and he describes his future to me.

On passthefellowship.com I read about a two-week cram course at an interstate, big-city hospital. It costs five thousand dollars plus airfares, accommodation and food. It starts on Monday. I call and am allocated the next-to-last place. I phone Ed and tell him. He says, *Two weeks? Five grand?* Then he'll only say, *Fine.* Blah blah. *Fine.* But blah blah blah. *Fine.* I phone Troy — imagining us sitting next to each other for two weeks — and he says he's in, but then misses the last place by ten minutes. Sunday night I pack a sandwich, a case of clothes and mixed teas, I squeeze Katie, kiss what turns out to be Ed's ear and get a taxi to the airport.

I lug my case into the beige hotel room. The smell makes me nauseous: rotting garbage beneath lemon deodoriser. I Blu-Tack the Do Not Disturb sign to the outside of the door. I Blu-Tack Katie's picture to my bedside. I wake up hourly to adjust the air-conditioning. I can't breathe without it blowing chill air directly on my face, and when my nose gets used to the cold I wake up and have to turn it down another degree. In the background is the usual big hotel, night-time symphony of stumbling laughter and slamming doors.

Close to dawn my room hits seven degrees and a woman in my dream holds up my high school class photo. She points to a girl in the third row. 'She committed suicide,' the woman says. I grab hold of the photograph with both fists and peer inside. I want to see the girl's face, I want to know who she is, but she blurs and slips from my gaze. She's my scotoma, my blind spot, a small scintillation over my macula densa. I wake up with sobs stuffing my throat. Every morning it's the same. I stumble to the shower, shove Vegemite in a roll in a bag in my backpack, throw the lot and myself out the door.

The early morning city is invariably pissed off. Cars try to kill me, drivers curse and spit, pedestrians slap me to the ground. I stumble so much I may as well crawl. I push ahead and wonder: how long exactly can a girl like me have stress-induced amenorrhea before she breaks a hip from her oestrogen-deficiency osteoporosis? I long for a walking frame, a disabled sign I can string around my neck, a guide-dog, a missing leg, *anything* that might force people to give me some space. But I'm the doctor and disease won't afflict me, only stalk me. I wait in a crowd for the bus, stinking-hot dragons knocking me over with their smoke. Everyone stares straight ahead, glazed, dissociated, breathing the fumes calmly, serving ergonomic earbuds with their nods.

The cram course is a bloodbath. The lecturers speak an aggressive foreign language to a theatre crammed with their compatriots. I am a tourist, jet-lagged and confused. I thought Aspergillus was a vegetable, Hashimoto a waiter, Kawasaki a motorcycle. I only knew MAC as the hamburger. Midway through the third lecture, I decide to leave after lunch. I must have wandered in here by mistake. I won't ever know all of this shit. I'm just masquerading, torturing my family. I just came to see what it's like and now I'm going home. Katie kicks into my chest, dragging a torpedo of pain. I have options. I strain to remember them. I once had a job in a department store. We made fun of people like these professors, with their paunch-splitting belts and untended beards, with their bleeding lipstick and painted-on eyebrows. It wasn't so bad there. We folded jumpers and hung pants. We learned the rules about spots and stripes. We created order with texture and shape. We took turns buying red frog lollies to suck on between customers. Please, nice old department store, please take me back?

In the toilet queue I stare at my boots, planning my escape, listing my options. Then I hear the other women cursing their memories, the college, this choice of career. They curse the difficulty of remembering glycoproteins, enzymes, catalyst and substrate, in the liver in the gut in the pancreas and brain. Every disease, its symptoms, its investigation, its complications and treatment. There is too much. They plan their escapes, list their options. I stand and listen to them pee and shit. Smell the rising miasmas of fear. They say, *Did you catch that bit about the Milan criteria? Do you get that insane formula for calculating positive predictive values?* They claw their stomachs and yank their ponytails. They twist the skin on their forearms, giving themselves terrible Chinese burns. I could fling myself into their arms screaming, *Thank you, thank you.* I could bite and lick their faces, then stand at the front of the lecture theatre screaming, *Everyone's terrified! We're all fucking shitting ourselves.* But I just pee really slowly, ears straining to catch the complaints.

Q 6.

What is the most common infection preceding the development of Guillain-Barré Syndrome?

(a) Campylobacter gastroenteritis

(b) Epstein-Barr virus

(c) Cytomegalovirus

(d) Herpes simplex virus

(e) Mycoplasma pneumonia

Troy's future goes like this: he wants to be a neurologist. Not an old-school neurologist, standing around with his fingers up his arse, admiring diseases he can neither treat nor cure. He wants to be an interventional neurologist. In Geneva, he will learn how to stick catheters through carotid arteries and up into a brain, where he will find and clear out the clots causing ischemic strokes. He will be fabulously wealthy and on call most nights. 'You'll have to marry one of those nurses you're always fucking,' I tell him, 'so she can retire and take care of everything else in your life.' He hardly remembers the nurses' names; recalls them by using the names of the wards in which they work: K3, H1, J2. Just like enzymes in the complement cascade. I imagine him sticking wires up people's skulls at 3 am, saving their lives, their memories, their brains, while his pretty blonde wife sleeps in, then fixes breakfast for their little girl and boy, piles them in the BMW SUV, drops them at childcare and springs off to yoga. He tells me stories: the eighty-year-old man – paralysed and mute from a massive middle cerebral artery occlusion – who, after his clot was dissolved, regained the use of his entire body and all his seven languages. He describes a brain angiogram, showing a clot-removal in real-time. He holds his cupped hands towards me, eyes electric. 'We're holding our breath, the left side of the brain has no blood flow, it's invisible, until he hits the clot, obliterates it, and then *swoosh* the vessels refill, blooming like a fragile flower, blood flow restored. It gives me goose bumps, Jess, it gives me fucking goose bumps.' I listen to him as we cram, drink and dream, and I know he will need that kind of springy, simple woman. Someone to smooth things over, to fill in any gaps. A nice Polyfilla kind of lady. And for some reason this makes my forehead feel like it's made of melting, wrinkled lead.

Q 7.

Treatment with ursodeoxycholic acid is most effective in which of the following conditions?

(a)   Primary sclerosing cholangitis

(b)   Microlithiasis with pancreatitis

(c)   Primary biliary cirrhosis

(d)   Massive choledocolithiasis

(e)   Choledocholithiasis with sepsis

When it is quiet and I am alone, I long for my little girl. I feel the empty cast of her in my arms, her outline hacking into me like a cookie-cutter. Even when I'm with her I long for her. I ache and I press her away.

And I long for a cigarette. I feel it between my fingers, white paper, smooth as lingerie. The tobacco damp and rich; a horticultural wonder. The comfort of smoke going in, coming out. My old friend, White-Smoke, filling me. Then the heartless bitch between my ears slices across my longing; she berates me with statistics, she beats me with pictures of hideous diseases, absolute risks, rotting lungs, throats dissolving into the mediastinum. Cancer cells sneer malevolent purple up into my microscope. My tiny pink alveoli tear and crumble, leaving me with hessian lungs. No desire can escape the knowledge this bitch has half a grasp on and I am alone with her. I would find someone to touch, for relief – *anybody* – but for the micro-fissures and E-coli, the urate, lysosomes and acid. Do you know how much DNA you swallow with a mouthful of sperm? How many chromosomes? All that indelible genetic material. The 25,000 codes that made their body, lying dormant in the salt. I can't eat that. I can't eat a code. What if it colonises me, like a virus, turns me into a chimera, a mutation of flesh? What if it won't come out once it's in?

If I'm staying at this course then I need to move. I do a six-minute walk test to the lecture theatre and arrive cyanotic. I bolt for an espresso at lunchtime but only reach Bruce Protocol Stage 2 – angina cuts me in half, my T-waves sag horribly. Maybe I've got HOCM or MODY or IDDM. Maybe I'm anaemic, maybe psychotic. I stumble through the park late in the afternoon, like a Vietnam vet shattered with PTSD. A council worker trims bright green seedlings with a chainsaw. A Tai Chi class breaks out into a fistfight. My bones vibrate with despair, and I can't remember what's in them: something to do with haematology, something to do with blood, something to do with cancer and chemotherapy and life.

In the lecture theatre I sit at the back and watch people jerk in and out of their micro-sleeps in between my own. I miss an entire lecture on the analysis of blood gases – a lecture I really needed to hear – while I stand in Yoshi Jones unable to choose between two bags. They are the same shape and size, have identical brass clasps and are cut from the same red, kimono fabric. But there is a subtle difference: one has a flower amongst the flesh-coloured embroidered branches, and the other has a cloud. I stand there weighing these handbags for ten full minutes. The Japanese sales assistant is nervous; she hovers behind me like a dragonfly. I want to tell her not to worry, that I'm not going to steal them, I just need to pick the right bag and I don't know how. I want to tell her that soon I will know, I just need a bit more time. I want to reassure her, but I have this decision to make and so cannot attend to her needs. I stand there, my eyes darting from one bag to the other: cloud, flower, cloud, flower. The bags are too small for my lecture notes, too small for my stethoscope; they're too small for anything but a lipstick and a cigarette. And my fingertips knead their soft, hopeful flesh.

Q 8.

Which of the following characteristics in a gram-positive organism is most strongly related to penicillin resistance?

(a)   The production of beta lactamase

(b)   Ribosomal proteins

(c)   Penicillin binding proteins

(d)   Superoxide ions

(e)   Panton Valentine leukocidin

Day three and in strolls lanky Irish. He folds like a precision instrument into a seat right in front. As usual, not a pen to his name. I watch his black clever head, the conducting system of my heart skipping playfully until lunch, and then I slush out with the mass, all headed for the sandwich table, and find him bent over a drinking fountain.

'Hey, Troy, you sneak in illegally?'

'Ho there, Jessie. Nope. Some joker didn't show up so they offered me the place. But I couldn't get a fuckin' flight till last night.' He smiles, punches my shoulder. 'How's it going, stress-mistress, have I missed much?'

'Oh God,' I say, my cheeks hot, my face stretched and torn by its grin, 'it's far worse than you could ever imagine.'

Troy laughs like I'm joking. 'So where we going to dinner tonight, then? Thai? Italian? Ten-dollar steak and Guinness at the pub?'

Q 9.

Which of the following class of drugs is most likely to precipitate the onset of Type 2 diabetes?

(a)   Atypical antipsychotic

(b)   Thiazide diuretic

(c)   Beta-blocker

(d)   Tricyclic antidepressant

(e)   Monoamine Oxidase inhibitor

Each night I call home and Ed puts me on speaker-phone so I can talk to Katie. I dread the calls, the talking into silence, the feeling guilty and bereft. It is far easier to be a no one from nowhere, some vessel for medical facts. But I ring dutifully, hoping Ed isn't campaigning against me. One night I'm chirping *hellos* and *I miss yous* and I hear the rustle of clothes and static. 'You still there?' I ask. 'Hello, Katie? Ed?' Rustle, rustle. And a bolt of fury splits me; I am just so sick of these strained silences, of begging to be forgiven. 'Look, Ed, if you're not going to even bother talking then I won't waste my time. How fucking difficult is it to say a simple hi? To let my daughter say hello?' And then Ed says, 'We're here, Jessica. Katie was hugging the handset. I told her you couldn't see her . . . But she doesn't understand.'

I take the book on congenital heart disease to the restaurant and lay it on the table, pen and highlighter perpendicular. Troy orders a bottle of Shiraz and three-dozen oysters.

'Does Shiraz go with oysters?' I ask him.

'What is this, the exam? Here, what goes with what is all up to us.'

The waiter pours the dark wine. I say, 'Did you know that eating four oysters supplies the recommended daily allowance of iron, copper, iodine, magnesium, calcium, zinc, manganese and phosphorus?'

Troy holds his glass with his fingertips, twirls the wine, examines the colour from underneath. He says, 'Eating oysters is like kissing the ocean right on the lips.'

I say, 'They're like a vitamin supplement! And all that zinc, eighty milligrams or so, terrific for the immune system!' I clear my throat. 'Not to mention the anti-oxidants in the wine. I mean this meal is *wholesome*. It'll probably amount to an extra month of life or some-thing!'

'Jessica.'

'Yes?'

'Drink your wine.'

'Okay!' I take a huge gulp.

'Just relax.' He nods at my book. 'Facts in the morning. Dinner now.'

'Dinner.'

'Dinner.'

I finger the ugly book with its thrown-together cover. But what's to design? What further enticement do you need to pick the fucker up and learn it cover to cover besides the thrilling block-letter title CONGENITAL HEART DISEASE? 'Right, well, it's just —' I look at him then back at the book '— I'm anxious anxious anxious . . . I forget it for a while, sometimes, when we're studying, but then *BAM*, it knocks me down again: fear I'll never pass, that I'm a stupid idiot for trying.'

The waiter places the massive platter of oysters between us. Troy looks at me, drinks long from his glass. He picks up an oyster in its shell, pokes the flesh. He hands the oyster to me and winks. 'Pucker up, babe.'

There is something deeply abnormal about sitting in a chair for ten hours a day frantically absorbing facts delivered in soundbites from the back of professors' throats. But sitting next to Troy, day after day in the icy lecture theatre, our elbows and shoulders playing gentle brushing games, is something else entirely. I can stare unimpeded as his quadriceps press denim, as his long Irish fingers grasp a pen. His body, hot with testosterone, keeps me awake, at the ready. I imagine his eyes on my thighs and take to wearing shorter skirts with fishnets and high boots. I cross my netted knees and I jangle my foot. I may not be good-looking but I can be chic. It all keeps my heart firing at per cents above average; it keeps me awake and absorbent. At lunchtimes we mingle with the other registrars we know, and with the increased flow of blood to my brain and to my skin, I am crude and witty and sparkling. I ape the lecturers, finger my décolletage, twist my hair round my finger. My painted nails flick and flash as I entertain the doctors with my smart-mouthed mocking, and try not to look at Troy.

A group of us eat dinner at a sushi train. We drink Asahi and sake and our plates pile up. Our talk is the kind of collective whingeing that I hate, and yet I can't resist: the exam, our work, the exam, the exam. Then a doctor from Prince of Wales named Andrew – looks about seventeen, eats his sushi with his fingers – gets controversial. 'I reckon any patient over eighty present-ing with a life-threatening illness should be palliated.'

'What?' I say. 'Even pneumonia? Even if we can cure them with something simple IV?'

'Unless their family can convince us that they were very highly functioning prior to the illness they should only be offered palliation.'

'Cripes,' says Joseph, a really nice, really fat registrar from our area. 'The hospitals would be empty.'

Andrew pushes a wad of pink ginger into his mouth, talks around it. 'We need to stop rejecting death. I worked up north for a year and let me tell you, the Aboriginals have got it right.' He examines then eats a carrot flower garnish. 'They accept death. They've incorporated it into their society.'

Troy looks angry. 'Yeah, sure they have, because they've never had any fuckin' choice. And can we please talk about something other than fucking medicine?'

Andrew nods. 'And we do have a choice, so the question then becomes how can you justify spending thirty grand to treat a non-functioning member of society?' Our bench is littered with saucers smeared with soy and wasabi. We are stuffed, but still we eat. We are drunk and yet we keep on drinking.

'How can you be an internal medicine physician if you won't treat anyone over eighty?' Joseph asks and reaches for his third plate of prawn tempura.

'My nan's eighty-one and she has her functions,' I say and smile. 'Anzac cookies, scones, unconditional love, the occasional financial bailout, I could go on.'

Eliot, the child genius says, 'But what if they're seventy-nine and three hundred and sixty-four days old? What if it's their eightieth *tomorrow* and they get pneumonia *today*? Do we give them one day of treatment then pull the plug?'

Andrew shrugs. 'I'm just saying . . .'

Joseph says, 'Hey, imagine the new market for forged birth certificates: "Fuck, that old bird sure doesn't look forty-four!"'

There is laughter. Troy pushes up off his stool, grabs his pile of plates, and heads for the cashier.

'Where you going?' I call after him. But he keeps walking, throws his money at the cash register and leaves.

I get back to my hotel room, buzzing with sake. I pull my phone out of my bag to text Troy. I'd forgotten to turn it off silent mode after the lectures, and there are five missed calls from Ed. I feel annoyed, impatient at the sight of all those missed calls. I ignore them and type in a message for Troy: *You okay?*

I stare at the phone until he answers: *Sure sugarplum. See you tomorrow. In our special little hell.*

I smile and prepare for sleep. I brush my teeth sitting on the edge of the bed and I catch sight of the photo of Katie on the bedside. I took the photo at a local festival about a year ago. She has a rainbow painted on her face and is leaning in to the camera, eyes squinting, smile a mile wide. I feel ashamed and trivial for spending the night dreaming about an Irish doctor instead of ringing my daughter. I probably have some sort of personality disorder. I probably have them all: Narcissistic, Psychopathic, Antisocial, Borderline – I don't love anyone but myself, I'll sacrifice anyone to get what I want, I indulge in criminal behaviours, I'm addicted to destroying all that I have.

I think all of this and still I am dizzy with desire.

Q 10.

Which of the following is the most important determinant of iron absorption?

(a) Shedding of duodenal enterocytes

(b) Transferrin receptor expression on enterocytes

(c) Hepcidin

(d) Haemosiderin excretion

(e) Kupffer cell iron metabolism

Lunchtime, week two and we're talking about running, something I know nothing at all about. Troy runs every day, for one hour, for two. After the exam he's flying to New York to run the marathon.

'How long's a marathon again?' I ask him.

'Twenty-six miles.'

'*Twenty-six miles?* That is just nuts, Troy. How many k's is that? Couldn't you call a cab?' I laugh.

He doesn't laugh. 'It's not about getting from A to B; it's about living A to B.'

'Running twenty-six miles is living?'

He shrugs. 'When I was fourteen my mother died from peritonitis after the treating team fucked around for two days deciding whether or not to give her antibiotics. It was the start of the whole resistant-bug freak out, and people were being incredibly conservative about giving antibiotics, thinking they were acting in the community's best interest or something.'

'Christ, I'm so sorry, Troy.'

'So she's lying there delirious and I just want her to die so she stops screaming about all this shit crawling up the walls, and then she does die and you know what my father found in her bedside table? Letters for me and my sister. She'd written them a year before, just in case.'

'Truly? Wow. What did she write?'

'You know, love and pride and take care, but she said this one thing that always puzzled me. She said that I had an *ethical* responsibility to myself to always do the best I could . . . I thought for years about that word ethical. I would walk around with those words "ethical responsibility" rolling around my mind. And when I started running I finally got it.'

'It's your ethical responsibility to run?'

'To strive. To push.' He leans towards me and I am scared of the ferocity in his eyes. He says, 'And besides, we live this illusion that everything is certain, is safe. It's rare for us to choose to undertake something that we may fail; that may cause us pain. We forget that to live you must risk something. A marathon is a great adventure, with a marathon you leap. You take a risk and you live.'

I wander back to the hotel, absent from the world around me, my head filled with two men. Poor Ed – at home wiping Weet-Bix from Katie's chin – looks anaemic beside Troy. Ed likes lamb and mashed potatoes and Buddy Holly eyeglasses. He thinks runners and gym-junkies are masochistic psychopaths. He sniggers when they fly past us on their long, brown limbs: their flesh straining and sweating, their alchemist cells turning oxygen into fuel. I think of Troy and feel sorry for Ed. I feel sorry for him, as Troy and I push on in our race.

Two weeks later I walk through our front door with thirty-four books of summaries and my armpits wet with guilt. I set down my suitcase, my box of books. Katie pauses in the hall, wary, then flings herself at my legs and hangs on. I look down at the top of her head and see a surprisingly large girl. I look down and feel nothing else but this mild surprise. Ed is a million miles across the hall, a smudge in a haze. I manage some form of greeting that involves no eye contact, peck the top of Katie's head and stagger to my desk.

I take Mondays off to cram. I study like a porn-star: legs spread up the wall, book in my crotch, saliva dripping from my lips and running slick down my yellow highlighter. I paint my toenails red and roam the house in my nightie. I call Ed at work. I make excuses for my behaviour – cortisol levels, adrenaline, stress – and I beg him to buy me a pack of 4B pencils and a bottle of rosemary oil on his way home. I rearrange sticky notes until he and Katie arrive. Katie throws herself at my study door and Ed knocks. I stick my hand out through the crack for the bag.

'Are you coming out for dinner?'

'I'm too busy.'

'Can we at least see your face?'

I open and close my hand.

'Oh for Christ's sake, here's your pencils. The health food shop ran out of the oil.'

I fling the door open and scream into his face, 'How the fuck do you expect me to study without rosemary oil?'

Katie starts to cry. She hides behind Ed's legs. I pick her up and kiss her wet cheeks. She flinches and writhes. I squeeze her protesting body, saying, 'I'm sorry, honey, Mummy's sorry.' I put her down. She looks at me as if I am a dangerous stranger and scoots behind Ed's legs again. I glare at Ed, slam the door, open it, snatch my bag of grey leads, slam it again.

Later that night, lying in bed in the dark, Ed spits, 'You're on your own from here on out, Jessica. Taking care of Katie is my priority, and I will do it to the best of my ability, but *you* are an adult and I expect you to *act* like a fucking adult, for your daughter's sake. And if you can't, then fuck off and do your fucking exam someplace else.' And he's lying there seething and spitting and the hatred in his voice is a heavy whip, but I can only note it, not feel it, as I'm marvelling at how he might as well be a character in a movie that I'm only half-watching, or a talking face in an ad, or a stranger I overhear in some café, on some corner, in some city I'm passing through. I have my eyes open in the dark, my back is to Ed and I'm being spat at, and isn't that a funny thing.

Q 11.

A patient presents with an anterior non ST elevation myocardial infarction, with transient T wave inversion in ECG leads V3–V6. The serum CKMB at 12 hours is 2 times the upper limit of normal (ULN), and 5 times the ULN at 24 hours. Troponin T levels at 12 hours are 3.5; at 24 hours they are 9.8.

72 hours later, the patient has further chest pain.

Which of the following best indicates recurrent MI?

(a) Left anterior descending artery occlusion on angiography

(b) CKMB 10 times the ULN

(c) Troponin T level of 9.7

(d) The pain is similar in duration and intensity to the index event

(e) Deep T wave inversion in ECG leads V3–V6

At work I find that I have lost all interest in my patients. I have to pretend to be a doctor. I am on my way to see a woman with a suspected heart attack when Amanda the ED registrar meets me in the corridor to talk about another patient they want me to assess.

'Jessica! Hi! I was just going to page you! I've got this fascinating old guy for you! He has CCF and COPD and a prior PE, so it's hard to work out exactly *why* he's *so* short of breath. So I did an ECG, a chest X-ray, a gas and got an echo. And it's *amazing*! He is *so* hypoxic on the gas, less than fifty! And the X-ray's really strange looking! Maybe failure, maybe infection, and his pulmonary pressures on the echo were *over sixty*! And yet his left ventricular function was *preserved*! And the prosthetic aortic valve was only mildly regurgitant! And so I don't know what's causing the extreme hypoxia!' Wide eyes, wide eyes.

I watch her and think: gosh, she's so enlivened by all this, isn't she. And me? I would rather be memorising the antibiotic guideline book I have in my bag, wedged between my elbow and ribs. I can feel it throbbing in there, waiting for me to know it, to push it through my retinas into the front of my brain. I don't care about *real* patients. I only care about hypothetical patients who may feature in exam questions. So I'm nodding and smiling, and in my head I'm screaming at her to shut up, screaming that I don't give a damn, that I just want to get on with seeing this other old lady who probably just has heartburn, so I can pack up my stuff, jump in my car, burn home to squeeze my prickly family, have a cup of tea and memorise the antibiotic book. So there's this

smiling layer, covering the screaming layer, all smother-
ing the layer of me that wonders if I'll ever like clinical
medicine again. And Amanda finally stops gushing and
stands there smiling at me with a kind of post-coital
glow and so I say, 'Thanks, Amanda, that was great.'

I walk into our café and Troy's at a table without notes,
with two glasses of red glinting above their stems like a
dare. I sit down and unzip my bag.

'Leave it,' he says. 'Tonight we drink.'

I pause, look at him and feel the pull. Like I'm all tied
up and his hands are around the rope, pulling me into
this fantasy world where there are no exams, no families,
no work, nor rest, nor anyone but us. Does he pull me
because he wants me? The thought makes me vertiginous
. . . then I remember I'm a mother, married, average-
looking, stressed. I remember he prefers perky blonde
nurses who attend BodyJam classes as if they're high
mass. All this push and pull and up and down, causing
micro-trauma in my coronary arteries, cardiac disasters
in my future. I feel pissed off, stupid, played with. 'Fine,'
I say, wrap my fist around the stem and drink the wine
in two gulps. 'So, what are we celebrating this time? The
fact that you are dead certain to pass the exam?' I rock
the glass, the last drop of wine rolls from side to side, like
aging blood in a test tube. 'And I . . . and I'm only . . .'
Troy's just watching with his impassive face and his lips
that crave Nurse, and I burst into tears and then have to
apologise over and over into his silence.

Q 12.

After a kidney transplant, infection with BK polyomavirus is most likely to manifest as:

(a) Aplastic anaemia

(b) Pulmonary infiltrates

(c) Nephropathy

(d) Progressive multi-focal leukoencephalopathy

(e) Haemorrhagic cystitis

Ed has an early morning meeting so I drop Katie off at childcare for the first time in months. I don't recognise any of the carers. One woman asks me if I brought a spare pair of underpants in case Katie has an accident. According to her name tag she's Fran, or actually, she's *Fran!*

I look at *Fran!* 'Underpants?'

Her eyes accuse me of heinous crimes. 'Yes. She's almost fully toilet trained.'

'She is? I didn't know, I mean I wasn't sure what she used at childcare.' I look down at Katie. I've never seen her use the toilet. She wears pull-up nappies at night. Pull-up nappies I've forgotten to change.

Fran sniffs.

Katie runs to the sandpit without saying goodbye. I open the door to leave, and I stumble. Righting myself, I look back at the nothing that has tripped me. Fran is watching, her suspicions confirmed. Okay, fine, I'm a bad, bad mother. But what about the seventies? Didn't all that happen? I stomp to the car longing for a name tag that explains I'm a doctor studying for her fellowship.

I want a name tag that tells that fat bitch she'll no doubt end up on my ward one day with her heart or her lungs or her kidneys and brains, and then she won't be so rude, oh no no no, *then* she'll wish she cut me a bit of slack, *then* she'll wish she smiled.

Q 13.

What is the strongest contraindication to the use of Interferon in viral hepatitis?

(a) Immunosuppression

(b) Hepatitis B envelope-antigen positivity

(c) Child–Pugh score of C

(d) The acquisition of hepatitis in childhood

(e) Portal hypertension

Two weeks before the exam, Ed and Katie fly to Adelaide to stay with Ed's mother and I stop sleeping. I lie awake running through the serological markers of rheumatological diseases, through my list of excuses I'll recite to the entire hospital when I fail. Rats die after thirty days of sleep deprivation. I wish they'd ask about that in the exam. How many days to kill a rat? Easy. The answer's thirty. But they won't ask that. They'll ask about proximal right coronary artery occlusions, about Wolf–Parkinson–White, about how to treat a pregnant woman with HELLP. I'll have to distinguish between the types of dementia, the types of lymphoma, know the use of a CTLA-receptor inhibitor. They'll ask me how morphine gets into a cell and how iron is absorbed in the gut. At 6 am I SMS Troy:

I'm so tired. Could it be cancer? He replies: *It's 6 am, not cancer. Try coffee.*

And I do, I try coffee, but what a pathetic stimulant coffee is. I stomp around the house swearing at my espresso. I jab the cup. *Are you the best I can come up with?* I jab myself. *I'm a doctor, for Christ's sake! Surely I can access better stimulants than this.* I call a shrink I know from uni and have him fax the pharmacy an authority script for Ritalin. 'I'll put you down as ADHD,' he chuckles. 'Oh well,' I say, 'there's worse things.'

Pretty soon I'm up to twelve tablets a day, I've stopped blinking and can see my apex beat pushing fast and strong against my ribs. By each afternoon I've desiccated my eyeballs and my head throbs dangerously. I don't mind the pain, I even enjoy it: it is something to fold into. I measure passing moments in little white tablets. Tablet tablet breakfast tablet tablet tablet lunch tablet tablet tablet dinner tablet tablet tablet tablet. After all, measuring stops things getting out of hand.

Troy asks me if I'm on something.

'What?' I say.

'You're talking fast,' he says. 'And you're getting thin.'

'Who has the time? Come on, do we give ACE-inhibitors to diabetics without microalbuminuria or hypertension?'

'No, we don't. The time for what?'

'To talk slow. To eat. And does Viagra work if the patient's on a beta-blocker?'

'Yes, it does. If you're on something you could share it, you know.'

I look at his melty browns. 'Well, what would you accept?'

'What've you got?'

I reach into my bag and chuck a strip of the little white tablets across the table. 'I have them, I have coffee, I have sugar. That's all I have.'

Troy reads the foil, looks at me like he's trying to decide if I'm a proximal or a distal renal tubular acidosis, and then pockets the Rit. 'In that case I'll take it, thanks, sugar.'

My skin is dry as autumn leaves and I haven't menstruated in months. I've reversed my sleep–wake cycle, but it doesn't matter because I don't leave my bed. I use copies of *The New England Journal of Medicine* as blankets, my course-notes as a pillow. I have attempted so many multiple-choice questions that I answer the phone with scenarios, 'Hello, I'm a forty-year-old female, previously in good health, with recent onset hypertension, tachycardia and a mild respiratory alkalosis. What's the *next best* investigation?'

It's the telephone company. A young man informs me that our bill is three months overdue.

I ask him, 'What's the *most likely* cause for our failure to pay a bill?'

'Excuse me?' he says.

'Wrong,' I say. 'Try again.'

He hangs up.

The phone rings again. I pick it up. 'Aha! Don't tell me! You have the right answer!'

'Usually, yes.' It's Troy. He asks, 'Wanna cram?'
And my degree of excitement is truly sick.

Q 14.

Which of the following statements is <u>incorrect</u> in regards
to mitochondria?

(a) Mitochondrial DNA accumulates mutations as a person
ages

(b) Mitochondrial DNA is maternally inherited

(c) The mitochondria in sperm die as the sperm matures

(d) Mutations most often result in defects affecting muscles

(e) Paternal imprinting can result in the non-penetrance
of mitochondrial DNA mutations

Two days to go and I walk to the supermarket for chocolate. I expect the usual fluro-lit sterility, but find the
supermarket's become a sanatorium of exotic diseases. I
see averted malar blotches and gloved calcinosis. There's
gynecomastia and Dupuytren's contractures, skin jaun-
diced and tethered, rashes that whisper a kidney's secrets
and fierce conjunctival injection. I see members of
secret clubs: SLE, Sjogren's and CREST, people alco-
holic, acromegalic and hypothyroid. I walk the aisles
like a schizophrenic: haunted and scorched, keeping my
X-ray eyes to the ground. I find myself near the freezers,
breathing like acute asthma. I text Troy: *Trapped in the
supermarket going mental help.* He texts back: *Take deep
breaths, buy your shit, walk home and revise baby.* He puts
two *xx*s at the end. Such pretty punctuation. It's the *xx*s
that get me out of there and home.

The exam is held in a broken down convention centre on the periphery of the hospital campus. I stock the car with two flasks of strong coffee, a bag of almonds and sultanas. We will work for four hours, break for lunch and then work for another four hours. Incredible and horrible that it all comes down to this matter of moments. I haven't slept and I caress my Ritalin and it croons to me that it will support me unconditionally. My little white friends will push me through the wall.

The exam room is chilly and smells of deadly, cold moulds. I wonder vaguely about the risk of Aspergillosis and MAC lung, but I can't take seriously the idea that there will be life after this day, and so I don't give a damn; I don't care if I am colonised with nasty grey mould; who needs lungs in non-existence? We sit at our allocated desks. I'm in the front row and Troy is in the back. The chubby administrative assistant, Suzie, hands out pencils and erasers, and runs through a list of rules as if this is kindergarten rather than the specialist medical exams.

I am happy that I only have a brick wall in front of me. It seems apt, and it will not distract me. For four hours Troy and Ed and Katie and I do not exist. I answer one question every two point five minutes. I guess and I guess and I guess, battling a sinking feeling that pulls me down and in, as if the only thing left inside me is a big, black hole.

During lunch I slide into the back seat of my car and lie in the foetal position chewing almonds and Ritalin, counting sultanas, sipping coffee that is still remarkably hot after all the centuries that have passed since the morning. I lie on the hot leather of the back seat, staring at the floor, at one of Katie's mangled dolls, *The Hungry Little Caterpillar*, crushed cookies, muesli-bar wrappers, my old notes. Detritus from some little girl's childhood. I lie alone – just a sheet of skin stretched over a black hole – until it is time for round two.

I walk inside, make eye contact with nobody. I sit at my desk and my heart beats in surges, pressing out huge volumes of hot blood with every contraction. I can hear the turbulence and it begins to scare me. I know I have taken too many stimulants and I imagine myself having a cardiac arrest, a seizure, or bursting an aneurysm mid-exam. Would anybody help me? Would anybody waste precious minutes resuscitating the doomed? The pass mark is not pre-set; the College has deemed that at least half of us must fail. Die, and you merely increase the other candidates' chances. Then I am best-guessing again, pencil to paper, etching my choice. A or B or C or D or E.

And then Suzie says, *Pens down*, and the paper is whisked away from my hands without a hug or a kiss goodbye, and we are piling outside into a sun-shining afternoon and this strange kind of warmth is coursing under my skin, like the hole has been replaced with lava, and there is Troy and he lifts me up and runs with me slung over his shoulders around the parking lot, scream-ing and whooping. And I'm laughing by then, of course, and feeling waves in my stomach each time he spins me around, but all I can think of is the feel of Troy. I want him to spin me round and round on our finish line like this forever.

Two hours later we meet at the pub, crowding around a table with a pen and pile of A4 to recall as many questions as possible for next year's candidates. Troy shimmers at my periphery; I'm hyper-aware but don't look. Three glasses of beer, our pens are in the ashtrays and we're screaming.

'*No way* it was Dengue virus, the fever came on *six weeks* after he was in PNG. It was *malaria* and you had to do a thick-film, not a PCR!'

'But he had diarrhoea *and* thrombocytopenia!'

'You can get that with malaria!'

'No *way*! You're far more likely to get it with Dengue.'

'But the incubation period for Dengue is less than fourteen days. You don't get Dengue after six weeks!'

We stand and point and spit and scream across the table, arguing for our lives. People at the tables around us stare and whisper.

'It was fecal *and* urinary incontinence, so it *had* to be cauda equina syndrome.' Someone turns the football down.

Eliot, the child genius, is chirpy and confident; punctilious even while intoxicated. 'But he denied his blindness, therefore that is Anton's syndrome: bilateral posterior cerebral circulatory infarct. Come on, you didn't know that?'

Troy, too, seems to have all the answers. 'It wasn't muscular dystrophy! She was spastic and hypereflexic! They were *upper* motor neuron lesions!' He laughs. 'And it was combined degeneration of the spinal cord, not MS – didn't you see the posterior column gad uptake on the MRI?'

I am in two places, split like a transverse dissection. One part laughs and points and screams. One part keeps track of Troy and quietly wonders what's next.

I stand up. 'I'm switching to wine.'

Troy stands as well and says, 'Anyone else want another?'

We walk to the bar, eyes ahead.

I clear my throat. 'What'd you put for the most common side effect of antidepressants?'

'Sexual dysfunction.'

'Yeah, that's what I said, too. Actually I think diarrhoea is more common, but I think the College believes sexual dysfunction to be under-reported, and more serious.'

'I'd have to agree with the College about that.' Troy laughs and leans against the bar, looking at me. 'So.' He touches the ends of my hair, twists a strand between his finger and thumb.

He looks down at my black singlet. 'You know, you have the most heartbreaking little vulnerable breasts.'

I look down at my breasts. 'There was a time when they weren't little ... Until I broke Katie's heart by starting her on formula.' Thinking about Katie while standing so close to Troy throws me into pixelated chaos. Amongst the mess in my head I long for the time when all Katie needed from me was warm, endless milk, when I could give her something absolutely and without ambiguity. And then my longing for Troy claws back under my skin like a desperate slut. I would swap her for those lips to want mine. I am drunk and exhausted and up to my neck in speed, but I think my sensorium is clear enough to know that I wouldn't give it a second thought, I would swap my own flesh and blood for a kiss. My carotid pulse surges fast and violent and I want to scream at his fingers: *Move to my face, cup my face, tilt it up towards you, kiss me, please.*

Troy takes my hand and says, 'Come with me.' He leads me through the crowd, all smashed together in the dim roaring room, pulls me into the disabled toilet and locks the door. In the dark little room that smells of disinfectant and urine, he pushes me against the door and finally we are kissing, cool and pure like drops of water falling onto a parched tongue and then hotter and more urgent, a torrential rush and women have not been kissed like this for centuries. And then his hands are under my skirt, his forefingers curled around the strings on either side of my underpants and he is pulling them down and I want him to do it, I want him to shove his cock inside me right there up against the cold door, but then I'm thinking that I am about to be fucked in a disabled toilet in a pub, and anxiety blooms – which ward will he allocate to me? And so I wriggle my arse to the side and say, 'Troy, not here, not now.' And he says, 'Jess, who the fuck cares where, just go with it, okay? It's an adventure: live a little, take a risk.' I push him away, gently. 'No.' And he takes my face in his big hands, strokes my lips with his thumbs. 'Okay, tomorrow, we'll meet tomorrow.' He lifts my face so I am looking at him; I can't speak with my pulse strangling me from inside my neck and so I nod. He says, 'I'll call you after my run.' And we kiss again, in sips, and re-join the group.

I tip my numb body into bed and wake up crying at 4 am. I have no idea who the fuck I am. Troy and the exam are fists pressed so close to my eyeballs that I can't focus on them. Anxiety and desire enmesh and my pulse fills the room, huge and red and suffocating. I roll out of bed, take out a clean sheet of A4 and at the top of the page I write WRONG. I should have written RIGHT or MORALLY SOUND, the list would've been shorter. By sunrise I'm up to forty-three items from the exam alone, I no longer have fingernails and I'm sweating beer. The pub was a delusion that has died and left me suffering alcohol's zero-order kinetics. I'm thinking maybe I could be a GP, a bartender, maybe even an English teacher – I loved my English teacher. Surely I could get a BA. I could start an ebay store selling all the shoes I've bought online in the past three months. I could open a school of dance. Do you need to be able to dance to open a school of dance? I lie on the floor next to the bed, face up, head pressing into the cold, hard floorboards. I start up a chant in my head: *Call me, call me, call me.*

Ed, yawning, 'What's wrong?'

'Nothing. Everything. Me. My answers.'

'Why are you on the floor?'

'No reason.'

'What time do you want to leave?'

'What?'

'We're taking Katie to the zoo today. Remember? To celebrate?'

'Celebrate what?'

'The end of hell. Your homecoming.'

'I can't.'

'What?'

'I can't.'

Ed, sneering, '*What?*'

Me, sitting up, spitting, 'I *said*. I *can't!*'

When they leave the house I grab a bottle of vodka from the freezer. I take it to bed, swigging until I feel something lifelike in my arteries. Watching the phone, waiting for Troy to call, I swig and swig until lifelike turns to a bubonic throbbing. I need cleansing. I need a three-week maple syrup and lemon juice fast. If I believed in homeopathy I'm sure there'd be some little white pill. But oh no, like an idiot, I *don't* believe in homeopathy, I believe in a paradigm I haven't mastered. I believe in something I'm too fucking thick-in-the-head to grasp. I need something raw. Something raw and beautiful. I am going crazy waiting for the call. I get up, kick my jeans around the room then pull them on. My mobile rings. It's Troy. He wants to meet at the bookshop café in two hours. We'll have coffee, he says, we'll go for a walk, he says, and if we want to, he says, we can go back to his flat, to eat. I tell him that's perfect, that I need to pick up a book, anyway. I leave immediately, blood–alcohol levels way over the legal limit, focusing on the idea of Raw Food. I park with a screech, enter the shopping centre and head for the 'Diseases and Conditions' section in the bookshop café. I can feel the cool, wet, skin-glowing goodness of pulverised carrot and shaved cucumber sliding down my oesophagus. Raw Food: the idea fills me with hope for a clean, clear emptiness. There is only one Raw Food book. It is from California and it's full of impossible ingredients and terrifying instructions: *Three days before you plan to eat, take your heart-of-water-reed and virgin coconut oil . . .* It's the gourmet version of *Harrison's*: cure by convolution. Sick of the impossible, I flee to the baking section to drool over déjà-vu food – tiny sugared violets, pale pink cream – until waves of nausea wipe me out. I grab a book by TC Boyle – *Tooth and Claw* – and find a seat by a window looking out onto a food court to wait for Troy.

Safe behind my glass I watch the living people mull and fuss. We are animals and we are not animals. We eat when we are not hungry, we drink when we are not thirsty, we form fists around chain-store shopping bags and tend our dead hair. I feel unwell and unstable, as if my blood has been replaced with rancid helium. Animate bodies walk to and fro with their heads sprouting tended, pretty death. Long dead hair and short dead hair, neat dead hair and ironed dead hair. I watch dead dreadlocks: blonde worms from surfers' skulls, and good on them, why not show it for what it is. I watch all these dead hairdos queue, load their trays, eat, drink, lick their fingers, shake little children with curly dead hair. I am fascinated and repulsed at all of these people with their landed hair, eating beyond hunger, drinking beyond thirst.

A surgical registrar I recognise from the hospital corridors, but whose name I can't recall, walks from outlet to outlet – daze-eyed, shoulders curved – studying menus. He looks shattered, most likely by a 32-hour shift of standing masked in a theatre, cutting out and stitching up. He sits at an Italian café, one of the few places with a sort of table service. I watch him, curious about what a shattered surgical registrar might eat. He orders, slides the salt and pepper to the far side of his table, aligning them with the edge. He folds the menu and places it on the table next to his. A waitress brings him two espressos. He sculls one, pushes the cup in line with the salt and pepper, and repeats this process exactly with the second cup. He does all of this in measured, economical movements, as if he's weaving a cage with fine wires. He opens the paper, scratches his nose, looks to his left, to his right, looks at his paper; all this fuss screaming of loneliness. The waitress carts out massive toasted sandwiches – bread thick, cheeses oozing – and enormous plates of writhing spaghetti. None of this is for him. People around him shove forkfuls of food in their mouths, eat melted cheese with their fingers, smear butter around their lips, their cheeks bulging with bread. His plate, when it arrives, holds a green salad. Is this what he imagined for himself when he signed up for surgical training? This sitting alone in a café eating pre-tossed salad delivered by a bored girl with ironed, dead hair? He folds his paper, runs his fingers down the crease, places it beside his plate, unfolds a paper serviette as if it's made of fine-grade linen. He eats without anything touching his lips; precise mouthfuls cut expertly with the café's blunt knife.

I look at my hands in my lap and see myself for what I am: alone at a table in a café, finding death in life, waiting for some guy who runs marathons, who calls my tits heartbreaking, who fucks nurses, who would've fucked me in a toilet, who has never once asked me about my daughter. It's fine to talk of adventure and of risk, of leaping and striving and ambition, as if we're utterly impermeable, as if all of these abstract, defensible ideas, when turned into action, will leave no trace. They are beautiful words that can rob you as they charm, like flashy con men who could never fulfil their promises. I stand up and walk out onto the street. Dazzled by the sunlight, dizzy with dehydration, as if I've just run a hundred miles with inadequate training, I walk away from those beautiful words. I am thirsty, so thirsty. I look around for a shop selling cold, bottled water and see a taxi pull into the curb. I wave at the driver and he nods, leans across, opens his door. I climb inside. The sun shines through the window, warming my skin. The driver turns and I ask him to drop me at the zoo, where I will search until I find them, those two I have lost.

Weightlessness

On Wednesday mornings my brother Chris and I were each handed two soft, brown one-dollar notes. We would keep them in our bedrooms all day, and then after school, walk to the milk bar and buy the ice-cream my brother had invented.

Sam, the Lebanese milk bar man, followed Chris's recipe. Take a milkshake cup. Half fill it with soft-serve. Add five long squirts of chocolate sauce and a scoop of crushed peanuts. Fill any remaining space in the cup with more soft-serve, more chocolate sauce, more peanuts. Chris would supervise as Sam made one for him and then one for me. They'd negotiated a price of two dollars. Sam had ordered in a packet of long handled spoons especially, so we could get to the ice-cream at the bottom of the cup.

When our mother arrived home from work we would tell her we were full, that we'd already eaten a packet of frozen mixed vegetables for dinner. When she sighed and turned around we'd flash each other demented, conspiratorial grins.

My brother was meticulous about what we ate. When I was sick he would make me bowls of orange jelly. When our dad went into the TAB, Chris would tell the large, hairy hand that periodically delivered bags of chips to us through the open car window, 'One bag of salt and vinegar and one bag of chicken next time, please.' And when he got them he took a chip from each bag and ate them together. He taught me, 'Now, Alice, this sharp taste goes well with the soft taste of chicken.' And in the back seat we played an endless game imagining what we would buy if we won Lotto.

I bought us a private soft-serve machine. He bought us an entire milk bar.

This morning I examine myself in the full-length mirror — I use a tortoiseshell hand mirror to see the back view. I examine myself today with my precise configuration of mirrors in order to view the aftermath of what I ate last night. There was bread and there was butter. There was bloody, juicy meat. Pale lemon tarts in puddles of cream, glasses of wine and liquor; more bread, fresh figs, candied oranges and cheese. Then Muscat and then whisky. I woke this morning, felt the flesh around my bones, and felt sick and ashamed. I see my body in the mirror: it wavers and warps and something intercepts. I am unsure what is truly mine and what is some kind of inheritance. I am unsure of the true borders of my body.

I stare and try to follow the lines that mark my borders. My husband Peter comes in, as I crane my neck, as I peer into my small hand mirror. He calls me by a nickname, takes my mirror away and gathers all of me into his arms. It seems I am crying.

Peter wipes my eyes and says, 'My sad Alice. I'll make you some breakfast. Would you like pancakes?'

I grab handfuls of my thighs, my stomach, my arms and I dig my fingers deep into the flesh. I say, 'I can't. Don't you see?' I look at him as if he is stupid, as if he is insane. 'Don't you see? I have to run. Not eat. I have to run.'

Our primary school went to the beach and whilst everyone else splashed and squealed into cool blue waves, whilst I walked on hard sand with foam between my toes, Chris sat on a bench in his navy blue tracksuit. He was fat, and he sat on the bench with his shoulders slumped and looked at the water or looked at his fingernails. He would never go swimming. I had never seen the skin on his legs or on his torso. I had never seen the skin on his shoulders. He kept it that hidden.

I run through violaceous air. All the pores of my skin open and weep. I look up as I circuit the oval. Clouds, like cotton candy beaten black and blue — bruised, deranged clouds — threaten rain. I run over cigarette butts outside the milk bar, on top of the grease stains in front of a takeaway; I charge through its fried-chip haze. I will never eat again, or if I do, then only steamed vegetables. At the corner of my street I smell roasting lamb: other people's family dinners.

It was only natural that Chris trained as a chef. His signature dish became a chocolate parfait with a tart berry sauce. Even at home he served it with two small, ceramic jugs — one filled with cream and one with extra sauce. He always worried when he offered me a plate. 'Are you sure it's enough, Alice? Are you positive?' And then he would sit and watch me as I ate. Each mouthful I took lessened his anxiety.

Chris met his wife at his restaurant, where the only things that passed between her lips were grilled sardines and menthol cigarettes. She was less than a quarter of his size, and her nose was as sharp as her tongue. After they were married, he wore even more clothes and his face was always red above the layers. I never saw him eat, but he grew heavier. She – almost impossibly – became thinner.

I peel off my soaking tracksuit and check myself with my mirrors. Fat necrosis occurs when flesh outgrows its blood supply. I am not sure what it looks like. It is probably black, or rotting and grey. In the mirrors my boundaries still waver, but I can feel my legs now; they are mine again. Exhausted, I lay down on my back so my stomach falls into concavity. As the sweat dries on my skin, I feel empty. All the fat is behind me – buttressed by my feather quilt. I float on a cloud; I am weightless. I can hear Peter behind the bathroom door; he urinates, then starts to whistle. If only I could stop eating, then I would feel like this when I stood up as well: whip thin and clear.

I am obsessed by the word 'sylph'. The word 'matronly' hounds me. I want my clothes to hang in a straight, neat line. I need emptiness.

I get up to shower and my head spins. The room greys, as if it is filled with fat necrosis. There is a fist-shaped gnaw just beneath my sternum, and my temples ache. I turn the water to hot. Peter joins me in the shower and I rest against his chest. We are torso to torso. Curly hairs nestle on my lips; the water is sharp and insistent against my back. I move forward a step so the water will hit me where I am soft, hoping it might help dissolve my flesh. Peter grows hard, up between my legs. I think, What temperature is needed for fat liquefaction? *That water hitting me, it sounds like a low sizzle. I start a list in my mind of all the things I am allowed to eat today.*

I can hear Peter breathe, he says, 'Let's go to bed, Alice, hmm?'

Water beats against my skin. I say, 'I'm too hungry now. After breakfast.'

He says he'll make blueberry pancakes, and I hit him on his back. 'You want me to be enormous. You must want it.'

And he squeezes my wet face against his chest, and the water strikes tile.

It was my brother's head waiter she flew away with. She just filled a suitcase with her bird-like belongings, and flew right away.

I eat four of my husband's famous, plate-sized pancakes. He has dusted them with vanilla powdered sugar. The first one tastes light and sweet; hot tangy berries explode in my mouth. Then I keep eating them because I have started, and now that I have started I am searching for conclusion. Peter hovers in my periphery, shakes the Saturday papers, and I taste nothing, nothing, I taste mouthfuls of nothing.

Soon after his wife left him, Chris called me. He told me there'd been an accident. I drove to his restaurant and found him in the dark dining room, sitting at a table with a blue and white tea towel wrapped around his hand. The towel was saturated with blood.

He looked up at me and said, 'I think I need a rest, Al.'

I unwrapped the tea towel, uncovering the deep gash in his skin. It was bleeding fast as spilling wine. I ordered him to the car, so I could get him stitched up at the hospital.

I almost crashed on the way when he told me that he'd cut himself on purpose, and when the cut wasn't deep enough, he'd dragged the blade through again and again, across the fleshy base of his thumb and up his wrist. He stared out of the passenger window, and quietly told me that he'd done it for the insurance, so he could afford to get away for a while. He kept his face averted, and while I drove I put my hand on his shoulder and missed a red light, because I had started to cry. People leaned on their horns; we were almost killed for the second time. 'Don't worry,' he said, 'Peter can hold things down for a while.'

I begin to calculate how many hours I will need to walk to burn away the pancakes that sit taut beneath my skin, and there aren't enough hours in the day. I am swollen and then skeletal, fat and then all gone. A blue and yellow weekend light reaches us through the French doors. Gravity asserts its tyrannical presence. I feel heavy in my chair. The orange vinyl cuts into my legs, fat bulges over the edge. I panic that I can no longer fit on a chair. I place my knife and fork down, and my shoulders droop, my chin sinks into rhinoceros jowls. I pick at a pimple, rub blood into my fingertips. Peter says, 'You're bleeding,' and hands me a tissue. I look at my bloodied fingertips. 'Disgusting that we bleed, isn't it?' He touches my chin. 'How about . . .?' He points his head towards our bedroom and looks hopeful. I tell him I'll meet him there.

I should not, I expect, want more; how could one demand more? Except it's not Peter at all: not his food, not him. It is something sick and unsatisfied in me.

For two months after he cut himself, after she left him, Chris lived in my house. It was just him and me. I was day manager of a large hotel, and when I left the house I was afraid for him. He was a structure of ice that might shatter any second; when I touched his skin he would flinch. I called his second chef, Peter, and asked him to drop by when he could, when I was out, just to check. Sometimes Peter would be there when I arrived home, always just about to leave, jiggling his keys around like he had something to say, but never saying it.

Chris stopped eating, but he still cooked for me. He watched me eat as usual, but now it was as if he too fed from my mouthfuls. As he slowly shrank, my fear grew heavy, insupportable.

Late one night, in desperation, I rang Lifeline and they told me to take him to a doctor. Peter agreed with me, and we sat there together trying to convince Chris. But Chris laughed when we suggested it. He looked back and forth, from Peter to me, laughed and said, 'Alice and Peter have got together and made a plan for me, how thoughtful.' He laughed in that bitter way only people who know they have nothing left ever laugh.

I take a walk around the kitchen, searching for conclusions. I pour a jar of peanuts into my mouth and chew, and I dip my hand into a box of crunchy oat cereal. I bend down into the fridge and find a tub of cinnamon yoghurt, dip two fingers deep inside, scoop up cold, white milk directly onto my tongue. I lick my fingers and open the blue cheese, have one bite, re-fold the foil, take a dried fig, then pick at Thursday night's pasta, cold from the bowl. I can only take shallow breaths, because my overfull stomach is pressed up into my diaphragm. I feel uncomfortable, need to lie down. I grab a handful of chocolate-smothered almonds and sit at the table to eat them. There is no thought in my mind. I stare at the edge of the fat Saturday paper. I am still hanging. I get more almonds. This time I put them all in at once, so I can feel them push against the roof of my mouth, against my cheeks, on my tongue. I gag as I chew, then I swallow and swallow. I drink tepid coffee. I am fit to burst. My head pounds. I check there is no one outside the French doors. I suck my finger and bury it, glistening, into the jar of powdered sugar open on the bench. Then I suck it clean again. I hear Peter call my name. Shame and regret sweep through me; a blast of heat.

I came home from work in the late afternoon and Chris was gone. Last night's dishes were clean and the blankets were tucked neatly around his mattress on the floor. I noticed my heart beat. I checked the backyard and nearly missed the fold of paper on the table with his thanks and his farewell. *I love you, Alice.* I ran to my car and – I couldn't contain it – a continuous, guttural noise spewed from my throat. I sped like this through the overcast afternoon.

The front door to the restaurant was locked. I ran down the laneway and through the back gate, my eyes skidding through the silence, my pulse distorting my vision. I yelled out the name of my brother, the name of his second chef, the name of the apprentice. I was breathing fast, so fast. The back door was wide open, leading into the corridor, leading to the dining room. Inside, the blinds were drawn and the tables all set in the coagulated half dark.

I walk to the bedroom and my steps are heavy. I lie next to Peter on the bed and whisper, 'Please don't touch me.' He asks me what's wrong. I tell him I feel sick. He asks if I need anything, brings his breath closer. I turn away with a sharp, unambiguous movement. He sighs and picks up a book. I cover myself with a blanket – a pale green mohair blanket he once gave me – and I grip my hands together and press them against my face. I am chanting in my head: don't think, don't think.

I wake up to a sharp afternoon light, sweat-soaked and cruel with thirst. The house is silent. My stomach feels bruised. I decide not to eat until tomorrow, and then only soup. I will try again to shrink in. I get out from under the blankets, pad to the bathroom and wash my face with cool water. I avert my eyes from what I may see in the mirror. I shake myself, will myself to feel my skin wrapped around me, to feel the edges of my body. I put on a long loose dress. I find a note on the stairs from Peter. He has gone to the restaurant, to work. I love you, Alice, a kiss. I sit down where I find myself, note in one hand, on a stair.

Chris was wearing the deep green jumper I had once given him for his birthday – size XXL and the exact colour of his eyes – it hung from his shrunken frame. Eyes closed, he was slumped on the floor in a pool of black. It was black, exactly black. It was black until I smeared it. It was black until I shook him, cold and still loose; until I left prints of it with my shoes, smeared it with my hands, as I pounded on his silent chest, as I ran to the phone – panicking, sick – as I held him, my arms around his big quiet skull, the both of us on the floor of the cool room. I sat in all that black and I held his empty shell.

And then there was a note on the restaurant's front door and a funeral of strangers. Our old parents came, as lost and dazed and distant as ever. The sharp bird showed her face, then fluttered away. Peter stood next to me, that same way: as if he had something to say, but not saying it.

For weeks I could eat nothing but packaged, sugared cereal, straight from the box. I lay catatonic in Chris's oversized clothes, feeling nothing but cold. One afternoon, Peter knocked at my door and I let him in. He came again. Then again. This second chef demanded nothing of me, and he brought me small things to eat: a chocolate, a cup of warm soup. Each afternoon he'd drop by, we'd exchange a few words, and he'd offer me these little morsels. Then he came earlier, cooked in my kitchen, sat with me and we ate. Him I could bear. But there was always something missing, something that left me hanging; an entire business unfinished. As if someone had neglected the final punctuation, or snatched away the last bite. And so there was never enough. He was never enough.

I sit where I find myself, on the stairs. I hold the note from Peter in my fist, and my brother, he has inundated me again. Like saliva flooding a mouth.

In Formation

For Oscar

My husband told me he'd become a Lacanian psychoanalyst in formation. For a moment I thought he'd joined a team of marching psychoanalysts. But 'in formation' only meant he'd started the training.

To become a Lacanian analyst in formation is a complicated process. The analysts have a meeting to decide who can start formation, then they decide, and then there's a ceremony.

I go to the ceremony. It is held in a small French bistro in the city. Five nervous men, two nervous women and my husband are all made analysts in formation. There are complicated speeches, then drinks. Everyone says, '*Yes?*' at the end of their sentences with an upward inflection, and a sort of French accent, although most of them grew up in Melbourne.

Everyone wears black, nothing but black. I wear a green dress and a red feather boa. I wear the boa because it matches my red lipstick, but halfway through the speeches I look out of the corner of my eyes and see endless stony faces and a field of matt black, and I am suddenly unsure why I have worn such a non-black accessory. I slowly unwind my boa and push it deep inside my satchel. I hope nobody will notice. I hope nobody will assume, extrapolate or draw conclusions about my character. I hope nobody will read me based only on my red feather boa.

After the speeches, my husband introduces me to the fully-formed analysts one by one. He says, 'This is my wife.' And each of the analysts looks at me from their half-open eyes, smiles a half-smile and then doesn't want any more information.

If they had have asked, I could have told them that I illustrate children's books. But maybe they could tell just by looking? Maybe they could see the ink stains on my fingers? Maybe they were so good at analysing they no longer needed to ask for information?

I smile and smile and smile. I smile until my face feels like an earthquake.

My husband tells me that Lacanian psychoanalysts still love Sigmund Freud, that He's still the great Grandaddy. He says Lacanian psychoanalysts are exactly like Freudian psychoanalysts, but with minor renovations: they are French instead of German; they use terminology from linguistics and structuralism instead of biology; and instead of fifty minutes they offer an excruciating consultation time that can vary from one minute to five hours.

Lacanians, he said, are Freudians with extensions.

They are Freud with a glittering new games room.

My husband's sister sends him a plastic Freud action figure from America, to congratulate him on becoming a Lacanian psychoanalyst in formation. She writes in her letter: *I was so glad to hear! I've told all my friends! My brother, the Freudian-Lacanian psycho in formation! (Whatever that means, bro!)*

The Freud action figure is made of moulded plastic and stands six inches tall. He holds a cigar in his fist and wears a black suit. The only movable part is his jaw. You can grab hold of the plastic moulded beard and make the mouth open and shut. I do that a few times and say, '*Yes?*' over and over in a falsetto French accent. My husband plucks Freud from my fingers and carefully stands him up on a pile of books by our bed.

Apparently, to become an analyst you need to undergo a complete psychoanalysis.

My husband's analyst is a bombshell who wears Issey Miyake and no lipstick. I see her give a lecture; she is short and fierce and plays intricate games with language.

She makes my husband tremble visibly and when I ask him what is wrong, he says that watching her is like falling from a mountain.

I look at him as if he has asked for a divorce, and he pats my knee and says, 'Don't worry, it's only my transference.' He holds up his finger. 'Resistance would be useless.'

I brush my teeth that night and I glance over at Freud. He is lying face down on top of the pile of books.

I snigger and say to my husband, 'Hey, did you notice? Freud has fallen.'

My husband turns and sees. He gets out of bed and says primly, 'No, he's only been knocked over by the cleaner.' And he picks Freud up gingerly and puts him back on his feet.

'Thank you, son,' I say in a high-pitched, Viennese accent.

My husband doesn't find that funny.

In the morning I turn Billie Holiday on loud in the kitchen and, while I wait for my bread to toast, I squint my eyes and sing into my fist. I scream, 'Lady sings the blues, and she's got it bad.' I play the trumpet solo on my knife. I use my breasts as drums.

For the vocal finale, I turn around and swoop down with my mouth close to my fist and see that my husband is standing quietly by the kitchen door, with his palm on his chin and his eyes staring at me with their lids halfway closed. Usually he would laugh and kiss me, but he doesn't smile or move or blink, so I quickly close my mouth, stand up straight and brush down the front of my purple skirt.

Now that my husband's a psychoanalyst in formation we have to go to dinner parties with psychoanalysts. To pass the time at these parties I play Spot-the-defining-feature-of-an-analyst's-house, and I notice the following: all the analysts have one Egyptian painting with lots of side-on eyes; they all have one room with Persian rugs on the wall and a mantelpiece cluttered with artefacts. The older ones have short-haired, orange dogs. Their music is minimalist and atonal. By the dining table, there is always a gigantic painting that looks like an explosion of blood. No one ever serves chicken or cauliflower. After dinner there is always a box of fat, brown cigars.

There are other things about analysts: the women have black and white hair and never wear lipstick. The men wear black suits. The conversations have many pauses. And they all nod an awful lot; none harder than the analysts in formation.

I start to see our house with new eyes and make the following observations: I made all of the art in our lounge room between Year One and the end of university. We do not have any dogs or rugs or mantelpieces or blood explosions. I own four different coloured feather boas and six felt hats and twenty-five lipsticks. None of my clothes are black. None of them are Issey Miyake. My husband has secretly bought an Egyptian eye painting and hung it in his study over the couch.

That night, I watch the Freud action figure from the corner of my eye and wonder what he would think about me. His mouth is closed, his face is completely blank and his shadow, cast by the moonlight, is massive against the wall. And I wonder what he would think about my husband's elegant analyst.

At the dinner parties, the analysts either tell true, third-hand anecdotes about Lacan or they talk about books. But they only ever talk about three books: *The Purloined Letter*, *Ulysses* and *Finnegans Wake*. I figure they are caught in a rut, so at one dinner party I go, 'What about that Raymond Carver story where he visits his ex-wife and then, when he leaves, he walks away from her through the street and the pavement is covered with fallen leaves. All these leaves, he thinks, so many leaves; leaves and leaves and leaves; someone ought to do something about all of these leaves.' My arms and palms are outstretched; I pause and look around the table.

Everyone is staring at me, frozen, like two rows of plastic dolls.

I hear a cricket chirp.

'It's really great,' I peep.

My husband clears his throat. 'So,' he says to the table of immobile analysts, 'that character Dupin from *The Purloined Letter* is pretty clever, yes?' Everyone nods and starts chewing and drinking and moving their forks up and down again.

I glance to the right and the left and then pick up my napkin and slowly deposit my cherry red lipstick there, the way I was taught to do with gristle. Then I stare down at my plate.

At home, in bed, wearing a tiny golden silk slip, I flick through their pale Lacanian journal. I get through one full title: *A Graphic Representation of One's Original Autre, or, Imaginary Axes Along a Really Long Signifying Chain.* Then my head suddenly hurts, and my husband's eyes are closed, so I turn out my lamp and lie awake, staring at Freud in the moonlight. I imagine he is standing guard over that mountain of books, like Moses on a hill.

Why did I have to say anything? I ask Freud in my mind. *Why did I open my goddamned mouth?*

Freud stands regal. My husband snores.

I go with my husband to a psychoanalytic conference in Adelaide. At the airport he buys me a bottle of Issey Miyake perfume. I stand there and smile like Doris fucking Day.

On the first day of lectures, he waits for me by the hotel door. I approach him wearing my gorgeous, beaded 1920s dress and my olive-green pointy boots. My husband does not look pleased. He stares at me with his mouth half-open and can't take his eyes off my favourite boots. I look down, too, then I look up at his face, and on the way there my eyes notice he is totally and completely covered in solid-black wool clothes. I look down at me again; the points on my shoes grow pointier, the green greener, the dress louder, the beads swishier.

My shoulders slump. I go, 'Oh . . . I'll be back in a minute.'

At home I remember nothing about the conference except for the following:

1. Someone used the word *identificofetishisationism* seven times in a twenty-minute lecture.
2. My husband still went wobbly in front of his analyst.
3. I didn't get to wear my favourite boots.

I look at the stupid Freud doll and narrow my eyes.

My husband starts staying out until midnight at seminars that are only for the Lacanian psychoanalysts in formation. He says he has to attend them all or else he'll get kicked out of training. When he comes home his eyes are distant and dreamy, he has cigar stains between his fingers, he hums to himself atonally.

Apparently, he stops liking the feel of my soft silk slips.

One night in bed he tells me, 'There is no such thing as *Woman*.'

I would say, *Well, that would account for it, then,* but he has already turned over and started snoring.

At home, alone, for the sixth time in a week, I don't feel like singing, I don't feel like dancing. I don't feel like cooking or reading or drawing. The only things I feel comfortable in are my husband's old, black jeans.

I pass Freud in the bedroom and accidentally kick him off his books.

When we eat dinner together now, instead of telling jokes and stories and feeding each other mouthfuls of food, my husband gives me non-stop lectures about how the unconscious is structured like a language, about how from the moment the human subject speaks it becomes fractured and marked by a gaping unfulfillable lack.

We go to another party and, just to see if my husband will notice, I decide that I won't utter a word. The entire night I communicate with movements of my head and my eyebrows. I only open my mouth to pour in some wine, or poke in some food. I shake my head politely when I am offered a cigar. I nod my head politely when the conversation turns to projective identification in the post-modern cinematic experience. I raise a wry eyebrow when they discuss the subject's desire for the phallus.

I drive us home, as my husband cannot focus. He looks out of the passenger seat window and murmurs, 'I am where I am not.'

I would say, *No kidding, Bucko,* but I am on a language strike.

The analyst-forming seminars continue and my husband stops eating at home.

On Sunday, the one day when there are no seminars, he shuts himself up in his study and smokes dozens of cigars.

I knock on his door at lunchtime and ask if he wants some chicken soup.

He looks out bleakly, through the smoke. He says, 'There is no relation between the sexes.'

'Oh,' I say quietly and close the door.

In the corridor I remember how five weeks ago my husband used to hate cigars and love my chicken soup.

I leave trails of wet tissues across the lounge room and up the stairs, but he doesn't follow them.

I am home alone again, in my husband's old, black jeans, staring at the wall above Freud's little plastic head.

'Oh, fuck this,' I say and I take off the jeans and throw them in the garbage. I put Billie Holiday on really loud, wrap my body in my four feather boas and dance around the bedroom.

I fill the bath with ice-cold water and push Freud in face down. I hold him there and curse. When I lift him out, the water flows right off his back. So I hurl him across the room. He soars through the air in a slow motion somersault, utterly unperturbed, his cigar held aloft, his moulded beard unruffled. He lands with a plop on our bed. I jump on him and twist my boa around his neck but he doesn't choke or splutter; he stays a calm, plastic pink.

I realise that Freud is indestructible.

I sit him up on the white pillow next to me in bed. In admiration I lend him half of my blue boa.

Freud and I sit there in the bedroom and wait for the moon to rise. We feel really comfortable together.

At ten minutes to midnight I put Freud back on his mountain, hang up my boas and slip on my silk.

My husband comes home. Dreamy and distant, he tells me that love is simply an illusion. He says, as if concentrating on something in the distance, 'It is simply the offering of something that you do not have.'

I remember that the last thing he offered me was his analyst's perfume. I struggle to maintain the connection, it seems to be important and my husband might even find it interesting, but finally, all I can say is, 'Oh' and he shakes his head and soon starts snoring atonally.

The following night there's not a scrap of food in the house so, on impulse, I pick Freud up and slip him into the mobile phone pocket in my satchel. I take him to the supermarket and I feel comforted to have him along.

When I'm choosing my grapes I say, 'Freud, what do you think about these?' and I lift the satchel's flap and hold a bunch above him. In the yoghurt section I consult him about whether I should buy strawberry or vanilla; in the meat section he advises me to choose the sirloin in preference to the fillet.

Then, Freud absolutely *insists* that I buy myself two big blocks of my favourite chocolate.

Then, instead of going home, Freud suggests that I take him to my favourite restaurant and afterwards to the movies.

Freud, let me tell you, turns out to be an absolute barrel of laughs.

We play an incredibly violent Japanese video game, then we walk along the deserted beach. Freud lies on my palm with his legs sticking out over my fingers.

On the beach, I hold my palm up high and twirl around slowly so he can see the ocean of black ink and the far off sparkling horizon. Very softly, very smoothly, just like Chet Baker, Freud hums me a song.

When we get home my husband is sitting on the edge of the bed looking nervous. 'Where on earth have you been?' he asks me like a housewife. 'And do you have any idea where my Freud has gone?'

I smile at him really sweetly and flutter my eyelashes as if they are butterflies. 'Why, Freud's been out with me.'

My husband looks really confused when I pull Freud out of my satchel, kiss him on the forehead and put him back on top of his mountain.

I yawn and say, 'I'm totally exhausted now and I'm going straight to sleep.'

The next night I put on my favourite green pointy boots and take Freud to jazz at the gallery. I can tell that Freud *really* likes my style. I put him in my top pocket and we look at all the paintings, then we sit by the musicians and talk and talk about everything you could imagine and more.

I discover that Freud is a *very* intelligent man.

And Freud, for that matter, thinks that I'm clever, too.

I can't explain why, but after we drink a bottle of red wine he develops a heavy South American accent, stands up on the tablecloth and starts to talk about Juan Davila. But he knows I don't mind, that I'm really rather flexible.

We get home late and I nod at my husband's worried face and say, '*Yes?*' with an upward inflection.

I make a feather boa nest on top of the pile of books and lay Freud gently in the middle, so he's sure not to slip. I say, in a singsong voice, 'Sometimes a feather boa is just a feather boa. And sometimes it's something else.'

My husband's mouth is gaping.

I fall straight to sleep.

I wake up fresh as a goddamned daisy, tuck Freud's legs under my belt and take him to the library.

He recommends I read the book of letters between him and his friend Fleiss.

I tell him that I feel guilty, as if I'm prying, but Freud tells me not to worry, it's okay for *me* to read them.

Late that night I lie next to my husband and open the book of letters. He looks over and asks what I'm reading. I tell him it's the correspondence between Freud and Fleiss.

'Oh!' he says excitedly. 'Can I have a look?'

'No,' I tell him, and turn over. 'Freud said only I could see.'

The next night my husband's at home and there's osso buco on the stovetop.

My husband says, 'It's not a monastery, they can't force me to go *every* day.'

Then he hands me a big bottle of Joy by Jean Patou. *My* perfume.

'Oh, thanks,' I say casually, and take the perfume to our bedroom.

In the bedroom I go, 'Freud! Check this out!' and hold the crystal bottle right in front of his eyes. I pirouette twice, then give him a little wink.

The next night my husband looks at me in and out of focus and says, 'How I've missed your pink, sparkly cardigans.'

Then he kisses me like a boa and carries me to the bedroom.

I tear off my clothes in the moonlight and just before I jump into bed with my husband, Freud and I make eye contact. I bend over and whisper, 'Thanks Freud.' Then I blow him a kiss, turn to my husband, and put my hand on my bare hip.

Fat Arse

More than 100 genes have been implicated in the determination of body weight. These genes, acting primarily in or through the central nervous system (primarily the hypothalamus and brain stem), affect conscious and unconscious aspects of food intake and energy expenditure. They include genes mediating brain sensing of fat stores, calorie flux in the gut, hedonic responses to specific foods, rates of energy expenditure, and even inclination to physical activity.

– *RL Leibel MD*

New England Journal of Medicine

Vol. 359 No. 24. December 11, 2008 p 2603

brain sensing of fat stores

Tina approaches me from behind, the way that she does, addicted as she is to checking out my arse. Hoping it's still bigger than hers. And it is! And her smile is genuinely happy. *How are you?* she asks, gripping my arm. *You look great!* she lies.

hedonic responses to specific foods

It had happened the way that it does, gradually, over a year or three; no time to jog, more reasons to bake cake, more money to eat out, to buy ingredients hand-snipped and shipped directly from Spain. Not to mention bad genes. And notice how everyone's an amateur chef now? And that hideous word, *foodie*? Nigella drools and licks and suddenly hedonism's legitimate. I simply stop saying no. Cream? Indiscriminate. Butter? Make mine thick and Danish. Cheese? Unmitigated. Chocolate? Let it pour where it will. Suddenly you have a midnight argument for the eating of cake: you're not fat, they're your sexy, luscious lines, and if you had a cooking show you too would wear Nigella's jewel-coloured twin-sets over extra-strength control garments – garments that kick your gut to your tits and your thighs to your arse, giving you a fake waist, just like hers. You can barely breathe with them on, and your sweat stings your chafing skin, but you'd wear them were you hefting your body around a set. But you're not, you're just going to work as the ward nurse on Respiratory, and you have to wear a navy blue and white uniform and so you don't wear control garments, you let it pour where it will. And it will, it will pour.

As a rule, all of my friends met me at eateries. And for a bunch of skinny girls, they would eat a surprising quantity of sausage rolls, lasagne with extra cheese and fries. They would stuff their bony faces with food dripping in fat, as if my bulky presence somehow liberated them. I would eat something small and watch them groan with pleasure and lick their knives and stuff their faces. *Oh, how I love these extra large flaky pastry sausage rolls, I'm so addicted to them, I might be naughty and get another!* I knew the next day, the next seven days, there'd be celery and carrots in penitence, but it seemed they had to pretend they could eat whatever they wanted. Or that with my fat eyes watching they were temporarily free to eat whatever they wanted?

Try it some time as an experiment: eat lunch with a fat friend. I bet you order dessert. As for me, I was always sitting at some eatery, next to some bingeing skinny friend, conscious of the double chin sliding down my neck, and trying to eat healthy, normal-sized food. Because contrary to popular imagination, once you are fat you only need to eat a normal amount of food to stay that way. Fat people don't eat five hundred pizzas and a trolley-load of M&Ms each night, oh no they don't. Once they have become fat, they eat just like you. Once grown, the fat is perfectly content to stay there in its soft rolls, untended, sworn at, and despised. Fat has very few needs.

calorie flux in the gut

But then my fat starts to melt away – quite quickly as it turns out – and I haven't seen Tina for six months, until one Saturday we meet again in the spot that we meet, out the front of Seamstress Restaurant. I'm leaning against the door frame, hands in the front pockets of my (new) (skinny) (tight) jeans and she comes up behind me, and she's not sure it's me – I know she hopes it's not me by the way she says, *Hello? Mandy?* and peeks round me like I'm a (thin) corner and there might be a murderer on the other side. Because guess what! I lost 32 kilos – enough fat to fill a wheelbarrow my doctor told me, and then laughed – and guess what! My arse is not big! In fact my arse is now definitely, unmistakably smaller than her arse. And she's not smiling when she makes it round the corner-that-is-me, and there is that fear look in her eyes, as if my arse *is* a murderer, and I wonder: why would my arse make my friend Tina afraid?

brain sensing of fat stores

Tina is very self-conscious. We all are, us women, but she has more than the usual quota. The only thing that would account for her degree of self-consciousness would be a secret belief that she is being filmed from all 360 degrees, twenty-four hours a day, and that the film will be watched by Earth's entire citizenry. And even as she bemoans some flaw or other, she is directing your eyes, asking you to look harder, to focus, to zoom in. *If only my upper arms were a little more toned,* she would say and caress them with sinuous movie-star finger-strokes. *If only.* And I would think: If only? Well, then what? And if I had asked her, *Then what, Tina?* she would have looked

confused, maybe laughed the question away. But I think
I knew the answer, the little arse-end of the thought she
kept in the foggy part of her brain. The secret answer to
If-only-then-what. *If only blah blah blah, arms/arse/inner
thigh, well then I'd be just . . . PERFECT.*

So we're sitting in the restaurant and the conversation's
stiff as a corpse and she doesn't mention my skinny at
all, until a guy I haven't seen for years walks over from
the bar and says, *Jesus Christ, Mand, look at ya! I hardly
recognised ya, you're so skinny!* And after he and I finish
our little talk, during which he keeps checking out my
biceps – eyes to biceps, eyes to biceps – as if he has
to keep confirming that they're really there, and during
which Tina sighs so loudly that I can hear her over the
re-remixed Blondie – after all that Tina goes, *Yeah, so
what happened to you?* As if my answer is going to be, *I
have cancer* or *I have leukaemia* or *I developed multiple serious
food intolerances and chronic typhoid fever.*

brain sensing of fat stores

It's incredible how invigorating it is to sit in front of your
friend and to no longer be sitting there as Her Fat Friend.
She will have the fear-in-the-eyes thing, alternating with
the don't-quite-know-where-to-look thing, alternating
with the I-no-longer-quite-know-who-I-am thing. Your
friend will be shaken. As if the world has suddenly revealed
itself to be a science-fiction novel, rather than *Sex and
The City.* And she'll be shocked and saddened because –
let's face it – a fat friend is a good friend! Ideal to take

shopping. As in (look of excitement!), *Let's try on dresses!* What an ideal audience you will be. How could you not admire her not-thin-but-thinner-than-yours ankles? How could you not notice her not-skinny-but-skinnier-than-yours stomach? How could she not feel terrific and reassured throwing open your change room door to ask your opinion on her midriff, and finding you bent over, bare lumpy arse to the door, stuck like sausage meat in a lime-green chiffon shift that's doubled up over your head and actually tearing? And she thinks you should be grateful; after all, she has such an expert eye. Man, ain't that the truth: clothes on or off she has you sized up in a second. Her sweeping look, laser-sharp, peels your skin.

hedonic responses to specific foods

And some celebrity says, like poetry:

> *I now know the reason*
> *For my struggle with my*
> *Weight*
> *I have a condition of the*
> *thyroid*
> *That makes me put on Weight.*

After all the inflation and deflation, like a balloon some kid's blowing, and after all that talking talking, chewing chewing, blah blah blahing on matching chat-show couches. After all the years of Hey-Joe-the-sales-skyrocket-if-she's-fat/starved-on-the-cover. After the size two, size sixteen, size two Citizens Of Humanity jeans. After firing their chefs for not getting the fuck out of bed at midnight to bake them a double butterscotch chocolate chip caramel honeycomb cream pie. After firing their chefs for fucking *listening* to them at midnight and baking them a double butterscotch chocolate chip caramel honeycomb cream pie. A *thyroid* condition? After all of *that*? Does a celebrity even know what a fucking thyroid gland is? Where it is? What it does?

Until that point I had defended them. So what? I used to say. So what if they're all fat, starved, uncultured, multi-billionaire Americans who'd sacrifice the entire African population in exchange for a bit of thin. So what? They have their problems too, right? And there are worse things, right? But to claim the authority of a thyroid condition is just so much bullshit. And it is such a betrayal.

brain sensing of fat stores

So what happened? She was fiddling with her chopsticks, not eating her pork belly, while I hoed into my crispy snapper. Chew chew chew, gesture gesture, fish pinned between my sticks, as if I ate like this every day. I told her I'd had full body lipo, that I had to wear a compression suit head to toe for six weeks, I told her they vacuumed twenty kilos of fat out from under my skin, just hoovered it all up in one afternoon, and it only cost sixteen grand and although I needed seven litres of blood transfused during the op and three weeks of intravenous antibiotics and a week in ICU because of staphylococcal septicaemia, it was definitely worth it.

And after all, I said – chopsticks around a nut – *it's just the facial of the twenty-first century.*

You should have seen her face: self-righteous horror mixed with glee, mixed with relief, mixed with gloating. Then I laughed and said, *As if, Tina.*

inclination to physical activity

I had, of course, looked into it. I'd studied before and after photos, made and cancelled a few dozen appointments. It seemed so quick, so simple. And it's not even expensive, when you consider the widely available interest-free repayment plans. But jeez, the potential for stuff-ups is immense. Allowing someone to remodel your flesh ... well ... how do you ensure that your surgeon is a decent sculptor? The boys at my high school who became doctors all *hated* art. What if my fat arse came out thin, but shaped like a turnip or a brick or a volcano? What if it was lumpy or lopsided? There are limits to the amount of Polyfilla you can use to plug up holes in the human body. These surgeons, with their weekend diplomas from the *Institute de Cosmétique et de Beauté, Internationale* were – right up until that weekend course – performing appendectomies, tonsillectomies and polopectomies; they were ripping out clearly defined, clearly diseased *bits*. And I've watched them bullying down the hospital corridors, like a pack of football thugs. Suddenly I'm supposed to trust them to re-create me into an after-picture I won't regret? And the detail about the blood loss and infections? That was straight from Google. There's at least one woman walking around North America with a cannonball-sized lipo dent in her outer thigh. And one woman's skin became so scarred and tight after her below-chin lipo got infected that her head is fixed in pardon-me-I'm-just-looking-for-something-I-dropped-on-the-floor. One minute you want a thin chin, the next minute you can't look up. Starvation seemed a safer option.

And I was, for a few months, always going to start starving tomorrow. But why is it that *not doing something* is so much harder than *doing something*? I could *do* anything: work, walk, eat, count calories, shop, worry, mull, abuse, drink, smoke, mull, worry, shop. But to not do . . .

conscious and unconscious aspects of food intake

Oh, you know, I told Tina, *I cut out a few lattes, quit daily baked goods, and, gram by gram, the weight just fell away.* I shovelled snapper. Tina swallowed saliva. A big gulp of saliva. Someone once wrote to a fitness magazine requesting the caloric content of saliva. My God, I thought when I read it, what's she planning to do, spit it all out? It's not fucking *sperm* (with thirty-five calories there's some sense in not swallowing). Anyway, we're in Seamstress and Blondie's still screaming her tortured-angel voice and Tina swallows her saliva, sets her chopsticks down, aligns them beside her bowl, and I know she won't pick them up again.

calorie flux in the gut

The first thing that happened was that I bought a small bowl.

It was after I watched a dietician thrust her fist into the air in front of her fat patient's face, as if indicating to him her desire to engage in fringe sexual practices. He looked at her fist in surprise – he was about fifty-five, wearing a cap and singlet, certainly not accustomed to young blondes offering him a fist. And then the dietician said, *This fist is the size of your stomach. This little fist.* So the truckie and I both got fear in our eyes and that night after work, I went to the Asian grocery store and bought a fist-sized Chinese bowl.

I'd use the bowl for breakfast and lunch. A fistful of something bran-y for breakfast, a fistful of greens and chicken for lunch. A bowl of coffee and an apple for afternoon tea. And for dinner, I went running. At first it was once round the block then come home to die. But bit by bit I could go further, die later. I was never hungry by the time I reached home. I was nauseated and exhausted, light-headed and empty.

Empty. For the first time in my life I felt empty. To say you are empty carries negative connotations. But this was no existential catastrophe. My guts were no longer jammed with digested, digesting, about to digest. My mind was no longer stuffed with what can I eat, when, how much, what recipe, what ingredients, and what's for dessert and for snacks, and what if that's not enough and what if it's yuck, and why stop at one oh please I insist, and what about tomorrow and Wednesday and Thursday. There was room to work. I could, for the first time, breathe in and breathe out without it causing me pain. I felt hunger.

I went to the doctor when my skin turned the colour of cement and he made me take iron supplements because

I was anaemic. He thought this was due to 1) a lack of red meat in my diet, and 2) something he called *March Haemolysis*. I thought he was taking the piss, I mean, March the month or March the hare, and what the heck have they to do with my blood? But it was *march* as in *marching*, or in my case, as in running. Apparently my generous weight banging down repeatedly against my soles – my tits and my arse and my gut all crashing to earth with each step – was squashing and splitting the red blood cells in my feet. I was *crushing* my blood. The doctor's eyelids spread, his eyebrows flew up. *Conga drummers sometimes get it in their palms!* he said.

brain sensing of fat stores

I suspect that people suspected I had an eating disorder. It's incredible, the way no one but your doctor and your demented great-aunt point out that you're fat. Even working in the hospital, no one mentions you are unhealthily, unattractively fat. But as soon as you start shedding, then the usual barriers regulating polite society no longer apply.

From most people, people I didn't even know, people I bought my bus ticket from, my diet coke, the woman at the dry-cleaners: *What's wrong are you sick what's happened are you okay you look skeletal are you eating should I be worried you're fading away have you seen a doctor stop losing weight young lady you look* GAUNT.

And from a certain type of girl – thin, usually, employed in retail, usually: *Wow you look amazing congratulations how'd you do it I wish I could lose weight how much did you lose how long did it take what did you eat was it Atkins or Zone do you work out cardio or weights how much wow.*

More than 100 genes have been implicated in the determination of body weight

There is research that suggests each person has a genetically-determined amount of fat they will carry. Apparently, once you reach that amount of fat on your bones then your brain sends signals all over the place to stop you from eating, to start you moving: your stomach feels full, your legs start to jiggle, your appetite dissolves, the thought of food makes you slightly nauseous. And if, on the other hand, you deplete your stores of fat, then your brain totally freaks out and does everything it can to make you eat eat eat until you fill that empty skin. Your brain, they say, activates powerful primitive reflexes, rendering you uncontrollably ravenous, insatiable, starving for more lard oil butter syrup chocolate sugar cake. Some researchers claim the brain's sensing of fat stores, its panic when they drop, is the main reason diets inevitably fail.

Researchers, however, in their white coats and goggles and latex-free gloves, huddling around bench-tops, discovering things in medical labs stinking of formaldehyde, have a special perspective and sometimes forget that the strictly linear logical chains – formulated in labs and disseminated in prestigious journals – hardly ever remain un-kinked in the human beast. And so, yes, there are powerful primitive reflexes to avoid pain and yet there is masochism. And yes, there are powerful primitive reflexes to care for your offspring, and yet there is abuse, desertion, rape. We should love happiness and yet we seek misery. We kink and kink and we kink. And so it is possible to revel in hunger, in want; to note the craving created from your own brain's panic at dwindling fat stores and to *revel*. The old pleasure-in-pain. And that is how my diet worked.

genes mediating brain sensing of fat stores, calorie flux in the gut,
hedonic responses to specific foods, rates of energy expenditure,
and even inclination to physical activity

So I clean my plate and say to Tina, *I think I'll have dessert*. She nods glumly and I order coconut pannacotta with mango crisps and black sesame ice-cream and I groan, and lick, and gloat as Tina sips from her black coffee. I haven't stopped smiling all night, but we are finding it hard to speak to each other, as if there's an elephant sitting in the middle of the table, obscuring the view, blocking eye contact. Tina can't finish a sentence. She is shell-shocked I know, my new physique repeatedly slapping her across the face.

I touch my napkin to the edges of my smile and chatter away about work, about movies, about a neurosurgeon I'm considering asking out, and Tina nods glumly and then we are finished eating – or I'm finished eating – and it's late-night shopping and so I say, *Let's try on dresses!* And Tina says she doesn't feel well and should go, so we do an only-above-the-tits hug goodbye, and I go to David Jones and walk into International Designers like a queen, knowing I can wear anything I want, knowing that there will be no troublesome thighs/bum/ stomach to distort the seamstresses' lines. I can feel all that food in my stomach and I feel a momentary panic, but I know it won't be there by tomorrow and I have the day off to jog, and these days I can fast for as long as is necessary, so I pick up a frock or two and glide to the change rooms, sales assistants trailing, smiling at me knowingly, conspiratorially, respectfully. I step into the flattering golden glow, my eyes fixed on the pale cream carpets and I strip down to my underwear and pull on a little black slip and step out of the cubicle to parade in front of my assistants. There are mirrors all around me, mirrors reflecting mirrors, like a maze or a kaleidoscope or an Aleph, and I try not to look at them but glimpse this girl, and she is so far away, a reflection of a reflection, and she has sunken eyes and sunken cheeks and her bones are hard and sharp and she looks like a starving ghoul, wearing her mother's giant black slip, and I catch my breath and divert my eyes and I smile at my assistants and croon, *So, how do I look?*

Blood

They were sharp shooters. They hunted rabbits and wood duck. They shot wild pigs, goats and kangaroos. They went away camping and came back sunburnt, with wild-man grins and an Esky packed with carcasses. A deep-freezer – the size of a car – growled against the wall in their kitchen, filled with headless animals in transparent bags: goose-bumped ducks, kangaroo, pale pink rabbits striped with rivulets of frozen black blood.

> *There are twenty-six polar bears in Australia.*
> *Half of them are alive.*
> *Half of them are stuffed.*

Bob shot his first animal in a paddock of high, dry grass when he was five. Rabbits were still in plague proportions, before myxomatosis made their eyes gummy and their little mouths bleed, before it was even thinkable that they might one day be scarce. The shot rang out and the rabbit dropped. Bob's father ruffled his hair.

At about the same time Anne took to removing the steel wool her mother had put behind the cupboards to block the mouse holes. Anne would push in cubes of yellow cheese and bottle tops of water. She couldn't just let them starve to death, trapped inside the wall. It wasn't their fault they were a plague.

> *There are approximately 25,000 wild polar bears in the world.*
> *Most live in the uppermost reaches of Canada, but they can also*
> *be found in Greenland, Alaska, Norway's Svalbard archipelago*
> *and Russia. In most places their numbers are stable or expanding*

and the bear is now classified as a threatened rather than an endangered species.

Since 1973 polar bears have been protected from indiscriminate slaughter by the Oslo Agreement, and since 2000 by a further treaty between the USA and Russia. Hunting polar bears in most countries is an activity restricted to indigenous communities.

At one time or another they kept dogs, cats, guinea pigs, rabbits, budgies, quails, finches, chickens, a duck named Rufus, lizards, black mice, a white rat, a lamb, poddy calves and fish. There were, at times, many insects.

Bob had bad luck with his pets. His fat brown chickens were found dead in their coop, white tissues stuffed down their throats. His lamb was frozen stiff behind the lemon tree. A horse kicked his dog to death. The neighbour broke his crow's squawking neck. His caterpillars ran away. In her bedroom, Anne had fish breaking longevity records. Bob's pets broke his heart.

After the death of each pet Bob would have a sort of fit in the backyard. He would scream, 'Why can't I keep anything alive?'

A polar bear's fur is not white. Each strand is transparent, with a hollow core, just like a thin glass straw. Polar bears look white because the space inside each strand of fur reflects and disperses visible light, in much the same way as ice and snow and a fine-cut diamond can.

By high school, the plague of mice had taken over. Anne's mother laid out rat baits. Anne heard from a boy at school that rat poison makes mice bleed from their stomach and their ears. They vomit blood, he said. They piss blood, he said. Their brains are destroyed by their own spurting blood. Anne found a glove, collected all the poison in a plastic bag, and buried it at the bottom of the rubbish.

At thirteen, Bob decided that he wanted to be a taxidermist when he grew up. A taxidermist their father knew from the pub gave him a weekend job. The taxidermist's shop was like a zoo: he had a buffalo head, a Bengal tiger, and a brightly coloured, $980 toucan that Bob especially coveted.

On Saturdays, Bob would skin fifty refrigerated bats and stuff a few dozen cane toads. The market for them was immense.

At home he started stuffing the animals he killed. The first was a ratty orange fox. He only stuffed the head. Its triangular face looked slightly wonky, mounted on a square jarrah plaque. He saved his pocket money to buy shiny glass eyes.

It was around this time that Anne turned vegetarian.

Viking hunters killed polar bear mothers, skinned them and lay the bloody pelts flat out on the snow. The cubs crawled back to lie in their mother's soft fur. From there they were simply plucked up and stuffed into sacks.

The polar bear's only real enemy is the human. Apart from humans, the polar bear stands at the very top of the Arctic's food chain: they even eat small whales marooned in the ice.

The garage was turned into a workshop for skinning, gutting, preserving and stuffing. Anne was haunted by images of Bob prying out brains, of him ripping out intestines. How did he cut through the necks? Where did he stash the refuse? She called her father and brother 'The Great White Hunters'. They laughed and said, 'Ah, so you're speaking to us now.'

In the West, the polar bear is considered to be the father of all hunting trophies.

Her father looked like a cross between Walter Matthau and Robert De Niro. Tall and dark, but droopy around the cheeks. Sharp, but a little eccentric.

He could make mouse hutches, fish tanks, aviaries, anything. When he made the chicken run, he hammered a nail through his forefinger. Anne held her stomach and ran to call the ambulance. Her father walked calmly to the kitchen, and pulled the nail out with a tea towel. He sat at the kitchen table and smiled at the look on Anne's face. He said, 'I thought you were going to be a doctor?' Anne told him again, 'I'm going to be a veterinarian.'

'Vets,' he said, examining his finger, 'perform operations, too.'

The only legal way for an Australian to kill a polar bear is to purchase a quota limited permit from a Canadian traditional hunter. The use of aircraft, icebreakers, traps or snares is forbidden, as is the killing of female bears with cubs younger than a year old. It is illegal to hunt near bear dens.

The house they lived in was a brick cottage surrounded by dirt paddocks in the optimistically-named suburb of

Deer Park. There were no deer. There was no park. But they had a sunroom.

The sunroom walls were dark brick, with a few aluminium windows and an eight-foot-high, wood-panel ceiling. By the time Anne neared the end of high school, the walls held over seventy stuffed animals, with very little space between them. One wall housed a wild boar, a woolly black bison, four ducks in flight, a pair of buffalo heads, a kangaroo from the neck up, a pet guinea pig, a fox, Peter their old blue budgie, and a pheasant with a brilliant yellow and green tail. Another wall held the Pacific Deer Grand Slam.

When Anne walked into the room, the effect of all this crowded taxidermy was overwhelming: such a deathly silent racket in her eyes.

Taxidermy preserves animals, at most, for a little over a human lifetime. You can tell the disintegration process has begun when the animal's hair leaves a halo, like snow, on the floor. Museums struggle against this disintegration: they control temperature, light and humidity; they condition and disinfect the air.

In 1991, Damien Hirst suspended a four-metre tiger shark in a tank of formaldehyde. He titled the work, The Physical Impossibility of Death in the Mind of Someone Living. *To the consternation of the curators, that $23 million shark is slowly dissolving.*

Her father was diagnosed with leukaemia. The specialist wore a suit, an expensive tie and shiny hard shoes. There was no need for a stethoscope. He held a family meeting so he could tell them, without once blinking, that their father had too many white blood cells. Anne imagined dots of pure white floating through her father's blood, as though it were snowing inside his veins, turning him into winter. 'In the future,' the specialist told them, 'we'll have to try a little chemotherapy. But for now, we'll treat conservatively.' They all stopped blinking. They all nodded in sync.

Her father still looked the same. He still went hunting with Bob. Years passed, and he simply had a blood test and saw the specialist every three months. Years passed, and he still pretty much looked like a cross between Matthau and De Niro. He was sometimes tired, but he still stood pretty tall.

> You hunt polar bear from dog sleds, led by guides. You spend your nights in a tent. You need clothing that will protect you in temperatures that can hit minus fifty degrees Celsius.

Bob became a panel beater, got married to a girl with honey brown hair and moved into a house not so far from Deer Park.

Anne memorised Singer, joined the RSPCA and PETA, and donated most of her pocket money. But before the Year Twelve exams, when faced with the university application form, her hand ticked medicine over veterinary science, her hand ticked medicine over zoology, it ticked medicine over animal husbandry.

> Your rifle must be utterly dry. Any moisture in the barrel, action, bolt, chamber or magazine will freeze solid, and render the gun useless. Ask a gunsmith to remove all traces of oil from your rifle. Ask him to pay particular attention to the inside of the bolt,

the firing pin, and the firing pin spring. You don't want to find
yourself face to face with the king of the Arctic food chain holding
a rifle that has seized.

There was a suspicious, meaty smell in the sunroom. The air in there was thick and dusty, and there was that smell . . . Anne suspected the wiry old billy goat: his ancient, indelible piss. But it was still the silence in that room which was most striking. All of those animals with their mouths open wide and not a peep to be heard. It was as terrifying, and as unrelenting, as the silence in a stethoscope held against a dead man's cold white chest.

Bodies are full of the tiniest flaws: flaws in the tissues, flaws in
the organs, flaws in the walls of the blood vessels. You are simply
an amalgam of threatened permeation; a haemorrhage held gently
at bay.

Blood is made up of red blood cells, white blood cells and
little fragments called platelets. Platelets are the plasterers: they
march around and patch up all the flaws. Platelets stop you from
leaking. Platelets hold back your haemorrhage.

Anne stopped feeling faint at the sight of blood when she graduated. And with that stethoscope around her neck, she felt she could probably conquer anything. She bought a dilapidated apartment and her dad helped her fix it up. There were cavities in the plaster and stains on the ceiling. None of the plumbing would work. They'd stand before some gaping hole and her father would say, 'Don't worry, we'll patch that up easy.' Anne saw him sit down at times and slump against his knees.

If you want to kill well you must aim for the heart. You could aim for the head but then you'll ruin your trophy. Anywhere else and the poor beast will just bleed to death. You must know how to send your bullet directly through the heart.

Anne visited her father in hospital when he received the first course of chemotherapy. Her father, in his pyjamas, in a starched white hospital bed. She bought him his favourite, an apple pie from Myer, but he couldn't even look at it. She fiddled with the IV line and explained that the doctors were attacking his white blood cells. He asked her if they were using a bomb, and laughed before he dry retched. She put her hand on his shoulder. He wiped his mouth and said, 'You want that Red deer, Doc?'

Once you have successfully killed your polar bear, you have to get its carcass back to Australia. To do so, you will need import permits from the Department of Fish & Wildlife, from Australian Customs, and from the Department of Agriculture. To get these permits you must produce an Australian and a Canadian Hunting Licence, a CITES permit and an export permit. The latter two documents will not be issued until you have killed the bear.

You can, as an alternative, hire a customs broker who specialises in the importation of animal trophies, and he will arrange the whole thing — except for the aim, except for the kill — for a substantial fee.

Regardless of who arranges it, the issuing of permits takes up to three months, during which time your dead bear will be stored in a Canadian refrigerator.

Anne holds a dinner party and unveils the Red deer. Her friends laugh and raise eyebrows. One wipes her napkin over her lips and says, 'Oh, you have got to be kidding.'

> *Polar bears give off no detectable heat. They are so well insulated with blubber and fur that they do not even show up in infra-red photographs. An infra-red photograph of a polar bear looks just like a small puff of red – the bear's warm exhalation.*

Bob showed Anne photographs: her father hunting for the Red deer, in camouflage gear, black stubble on his jaw and a gun slung over his shoulder. He'd camped for two weeks, waiting. They were at one of those family dinners, feeling dazed and raw and numb. The world was vertiginous, not altogether real. Then someone pulled out a box of old photographs. And they peered into shards of clarity.

> *Polar bears are the toughest animals on earth to bring down. Only the most skilled hunters even attempt it. Fewer than ten per cent get their bear.*

Bob reads about the polar bear in the Deer Park newspaper. The article, illustrated with a picture of the animal, announces the auction of a deceased estate. The bear – forefeet outstretched, mouth open wide – towers in someone's lounge room, next to a small, framed print.

Bob calls Anne without thinking, his voice wavery and excited, like when they were kids, after too many lollies. 'Can you believe it?' he asks her. 'A polar bear. Only ten k's from here!'

On the day of the auction Anne goes to work and keeps her phone in her pocket. She investigates fevers, shortness of breath, an exacerbation of pain in one man's chest. She adds and subtracts drugs with a hopeful precision. When her brother rings in the afternoon she holds her phone with both hands, presses it to her ear. 'Did you get it?' She imagines being able to wrap her arms around its massive body and bury her face in its soft fur.

For a while they hold on to their phones in silence. Anne hears Bob take in a long, jagged breath.

Grief is the way you keep a lost object present in your world. In exchange for some pain, grieving keeps them with you for just a little longer, frozen and stable as hard blue ice.

Grief is preservation.

Anne writes to an Arctic safari operator in Canada.

Rick, she writes, *I would like to arrange for my brother to hunt a polar bear.*

She imagines what it must be like to shoot a gun. The weight of it, the power. To have that metal up close to her face, and the trigger beneath her finger. To squint through the scope and see only the animal she wants to kill.

The Arctic is so white. It's as white as the corner of a young girl's eye. As white as sharp, bright light. As the after-flash of loneliness.

The chemotherapy slipped into her father's bone marrow and wiped out everything that moved. White blood cells, red blood cells, platelets, everything. When he ran out of platelets, he started to bleed. Like a glass full of warm blood, shattering.

Now Anne has a thought about what happened to her father. The thought barges in like a redneck, and guts her with its arrival: *I let them use a bomb.*

> *And the Arctic is blue. As blue as wind. As blue as cold, deep water. As pale, pale blue as a melancholy thought that follows you like vapour.*

She closes her eyes and he looms up large. He fills her mind and leaks out between her eyelids like fine-cut diamonds, like ice, like snow.

One Down

Dad left us in kindergarten.

'Fiona,' he crouched down and said. 'Fifi. I'll see you real soon, baby-doll.'

'Real soon', I wondered, what's 'real soon'? Was it maybe the opposite of 'false soon'?

Mum was a wreck so I stayed at Nan's, sharing her doona and her queen-sized bed. We'd snuggle up and Nan would tell me, 'Men never ever know what they want. They need us to tell them, they need us to make all their plans.'

By the time I went home, Mum's eyes and face had narrowed, and she went around muttering, 'Men only ever want one thing. Watch out for men, Fiona. They only ever want *one thing*.'

I was understandably confused. Men didn't know what they wanted; men knew what they wanted, and that was one thing. I was only sure about two things. Men – that is, Dad – seemed to know pretty clearly what they *didn't* want: us. And 'real soon' turned out to be the opposite of 'soon'.

Primary School

Primary school was marked by crushes: multiple, arbitrary, and always unrequited. David for his coloured pencils, Doug for his blond hair, Stephen for his one invitation for me to play kiss-chasey. And even more painful: Mr Bridge for his smile, Mr Jackson for the guitar lessons, and Mr Tomford for his knowledge of the atlas. They all made me go faster: my breath, my pulse, my walk. I spent six years speeding around, dreaming of my crushes, and from about Year Five-and-a-half, getting strange feelings in my undies when I imagined them having a crush back on me.

Of course they never did. They didn't notice my moon eyes, my new red cardigan, the fact that I loitered around about one step behind them. I was the smallest girl in the class and I had to wear glasses, but I wasn't an ant, and yet I was so far below the boys' radars, I may as well have been. They all had *their* moon eyes directed at Miss Beveridge and her river of glossy black hair, at Miss Fletcher's cleavage, at Karena and Danielle's little arses, cupped in tight new jeans. But still, I continued to hope. I continued to wait and to hope and to dream inside my cardigans. *One day,* I thought, *one day they'll notice.* I must have *some* way of giving them a plan; *something* I can tell them to want. Miss Beveridge's hair told them, Miss Fletcher's cleavage told them, as did Karena and Danielle's arses. All of those girls had something that said to the boys, 'You want this.' I just didn't have anything that would tell.

Secondary School

Twelve years old, finally starting high school and never been kissed: it was written all over me.

'Watch out for those boys,' my mum told me, butting out a cigarette in the Buckingham Palace ashtray. 'They'll hold you hostage, get you pregnant and then drop you like a hot potato.'

Being held hostage sounded better than being ignored, but perhaps it only looked that way from this side of the fence. Mum lit another cigarette. 'Remember this, Fiona.' She inhaled and exhaled. 'Men are immature beasts who control the world. They only want *one thing*. Don't give them the time of day.'

High school was fine. I knew a bunch of kids from Year Six, the teachers were grumpier but smarter, and I was still the smallest girl in class. My mum started giving me five dollars a week pocket money in exchange for me cooking dinner. Apparently that was a small fortune. I could spend it as I wished, no questions asked: clarinet lessons, pens, art and craft supplies, lollies, cigarettes, magazines. I didn't have an instrument, and hated art and craft, so each week I went to the newsagents to research men. Mostly, I bought *Dolly* magazine.

After School

So one weekend I'm reading *Dolly* and there's this letter from a Maria G.

> Dear Dolly,
> I am a Catholic and I plan to marry in May. I have been masturbating since I turned 15. I've tried to stop, but can't. Does this mean I'm no longer a virgin? Will my husband be able to tell on our wedding night?
> Worried,
> Maria G

I took the letter to the kitchen. 'Hey, Mum,' I said. 'What's masturbating?'

She spun her head round really fast, her hands no longer rubbing dishcloth against dish. 'What?' I pressed my finger against Maria G's letter and passed her *Dolly*. Mum put the dish down, slung the cloth over her shoulder and grabbed the mag. Her brow furrowed and her lips moved as she read, until they froze and then pursed, in that way that caused me physical pain. She looked at me and rolled the magazine into a club. She rammed the magazine into my chest. 'Where'd you get this rot?' she said. 'The girl's a stupid, *stupid* idiot.' Then she stormed off to throw *Dolly* into the bin.

Dolly only took me so far. I really wanted to buy *Cleo*. *Cleo* still carried a shroud of soft porn, even though they'd discarded the male centrefolds around the same time moustaches turned gay. I went to the newsagents on pocket money day with a plan to buy *Cleo*. But instead, I wandered round and round the magazine displays, eyeing *Cleo* each time I passed and not picking it up. Round and round I went, eyeing the bloke behind the counter, wondering if a pack of chewie would distract him from the fact that I was buying that-mag-that-used-to-carry-pictures-of-dicks. Another lap. There was a woman on *Cleo*'s cover with long blonde hair, parted lips, fingers caressing her thighs. On *Dolly*, pigtails sandwiched cheesy grins. *Dolly* was cute; *Cleo* was something else. The newsagent micro-flicked his eyes on then off my navy jumper and he didn't take a second look. I grabbed *Cleo* and slung her onto the counter.

What I Needed Was In June

The information from *Cleo*, coupled with what I picked up at school, gradually led to a few important realisations.

Dressing cute does not tell a boy what to do. Dressing cool does not give a boy a plan. To get a boy to want-you-like-a-One-Thing you have to wear clothes that cup and pull and reveal, even if what's underneath is not so crash-hot. You didn't need much clothing to tell a boy what to do. In the local op shop I bought a black denim skirt – so short it was almost a belt – and a handful of T-shirts four sizes too small.

But it was difficult for me to wear clothes that would tell a boy what to do when I lived with a mother who refused to let me out of the house because I looked, quote, like a tart. I would've liked to point out to her that I didn't see a crowd of men pushing against the front door to get to *her*. That, in fact, I hadn't seen a single guy swing by to see her since Dad swung away. But I knew that where my mother was concerned, logical discussions were generally counter-productive. *Cleo* suggested layers: *Outfits that take you from work to play!* Or, in my case, top layers that got me out the door.

So I pulled on my gear and then hid it under an oversized jacket and hippy skirt. I walked out the front door to the bus stop, slipped out of the jacket and long skirt and into a brand new world where I was, all of a sudden, visible.

I stayed with my grandmother a few times a week, as I had since I was a kid; the only difference now being our separate beds, and my understanding that Nan's imagination was astonishingly retarded. 'Ignorance,' her favourite saying went, 'is bliss.' This gave me immense freedom: I could dress as I pleased, and keep my growing collection of *Cleo*s under my bed, knowing she'd never disturb their covers. One weekend, I kissed her goodnight, propped myself up in bed and opened June. June, it turned out, had a sealed section on masturbation. The talk was all about orgasms, about setting your body free, about totally-losing-control. This was the point of orgasms, and orgasms were the point of masturbation. It was, June said, easier to learn to have orgasms by yourself, until you felt comfortable enough to let someone else do it for you, until you felt comfortable enough to let someone else take control. There were pictures of vibrators and plastic spikes and double-headed scary things I didn't want to think too much about. But you didn't need the paraphernalia to get an orgasm, all you needed was one finger and your own fleshy outsprout; every girl had one of them, and they'd drawn a map. I studied their map and steered my one finger into port. And Maria G and hallelujah.

The Real Thing

A few weeks later I was in the back seat of a silver Mercedes, sitting next to Erik, the Swedish exchange student. Erik, Swedish, exchange student – you can imagine what he looked like, one of those clichés that turns out to be true. And I decided to have sex with him, and then with a man from every country in the world. I stared straight ahead into the pale brown curls of his host mother's hairdo, feeling my borders for the first time, swollen with new ambition. I smoothed and smoothed my skirt over the tops of my thighs (thus, Erik got told what to do) and I saw myself in the back seat of a silver car, speeding down a cool, dark highway; a girl with long black hair, a barely-there T-shirt, and a plan I would impose on a whole world of boys.

Erik

Turns out Erik, the Swedish exchange student, had a really long, really thin dick. I could feel it pushing my cervix up into whatever was above a cervix.

My grandmother would've had a heart attack. She thought Erik was a nice boy. *She* suggested I stay at Vera and Frank's house and, in the morning, show Erik the zoo. She imagined we'd sleep with expectant smiles on our faces, dreaming of lions and butterflies and ice-cream. If someone had told her Erik was going to shove his long, thin dick inside her twelve-year-old granddaughter she would have looked confused – as if a crowd of angry men were screaming at her in Chinese – then her jaw would've gone slack, signalling the heart attack.

So Erik pumped away, thin and sweatless, and I looked up at where the ceiling would've been if it wasn't so dark, and I thought: *One Down*.

Australia

I covered Australia soon after. At a party, wedged between a wall and some kid's parents' bed. Every now and then someone would come in and watch. It was my lace crop-top that told that one what to do. I didn't catch his name, but the Australian was pissed and hot and went as fast as he could, unable to believe his luck, thinking it was *his* plan he was enacting. His hair was brown and his sweat stank of Brandivino and that's pretty much all I can tell you.

The next morning the insides of my legs hurt right up inside me, like carpet burn. Each step I took caused me pain, reminding me of the little mermaid from the fairytale. This made me sad momentarily, so I consoled myself by contemplating my grand plan and humming: *Two Down, Two Down.*

I heard afterwards that Australia was relieved to hear I wasn't an ugly bitch, and to be perfectly honest, I was relieved, too. I'd heard people say that I looked like my dad. When it was mentioned, my mum acted as if it was a terrible insult. I'd seen photos of him: he looked like a bloke with brown hair. I'd studied myself in the mirror, trying to put two and two together (eyes and nose, plus mouth and ears) and I didn't look like a bloke, that bloke, or any old bloke. And my hair was black. But still, who was I to say? So it was a relief to know that despite maybe looking like my dad, the family-deserting-gorilla-who-only-ever-wanted-one-thing, I wasn't an ugly bitch. Frank ugliness may have made my task difficult, despite the *Cleo* clothes.

School

After that party, the girls at the good-school-that-cost-a-fortune I bussed to each day stayed a few steps behind me.

They dropped their cupped palms and stopped whispering when I turned around. Suddenly Melinda – who'd previously claimed to have lost it on a park bench with a guy named Leaf – was a virgin again. Suddenly, I was the only one who wasn't. As long as I wasn't looking, they watched me: searching for changes, or for blood, or for something. I hitched my schoolbag high up on my bare shoulder, wrapped my knuckles around both straps and left the girls trailing behind. *They* couldn't give plan anywhere near as good as me.

Second Generation

Things stagnated at Two Down for a couple of years. I kissed Eddie (a second-generation Maltese) at every Blue Light Disco, but apart from that I was just busy with Year Eight stuff: reading *Jane Eyre*, trampolining, my finger, learning to inhale. All the boys in my neighbourhood were Aussies or second-generation Maltese. I'd decided that second-generation didn't count. Eddie didn't know it, but my decision regarding the second generations had a significant impact on the course of his adolescence. Poor Eddie: I gave him plan after plan and would never let him follow through.

America

Year Ten. Fifteen years old and in the prime of my life and this American boy gets a job as teacher's assistant in European History. He was sort of hairy, but in a golden kind of way so I didn't really mind, and it turns out that if you do it sitting up there's not that much skin-to-hair contact, anyway. So I wore a short red dress that told him exactly what to do, and Three Down happened one lunchtime. After I wiped myself, pulled my undies back up and went to unlock the toilet door, his tan skin turned totally white. It was the first time I'd actually seen that happen. You read about it all the time and figure it's just a metaphor, but it's not, it's real. I thought: *Cool.*

He looked from my face to the lock, from my face to the lock, and then down at his, well, let's just say he looked down at his lap area. Then he threw his face into his hands and crouched right over. 'What have I done?' he moaned, in American. 'What have I done?'

It's funny how they always believe it's them that have done something, isn't it? I patted his golden head. 'You'll be okay,' I crooned. 'You'll be just fine.' Pat pat pat. Then I walked out, sat on the grass in the middle of the oval and ate the rest of my peanut butter sandwich. The sun toasted the crown of my head and I thought: *Three Down, Three Down, Three Down.*

Moleskine

I decided to pin a few things down. Turns out the exact number of countries in the world is controversial. Almost all the countries-who-recognise-countries in the world recognise one hundred and ninety-five countries. The exception is America, who will only recognise one hundred and ninety-three countries. I wondered if it would be a good thing or a bad thing to remain unrecognised by America? I decided to recognise the two rejected countries. I figured I had till I was thirty, at which time old age would set in, so that meant I needed 12.8 successful interactions a year – one a month, give or take. I bought a small red notebook to keep tabs. It was a Moleskine; the one they say Hemingway used.

Africa

Melbourne's renovated Flinders Street Station was a good place to meet boys. They'd recently closed the fish and chip shop, ripped out the benches, put in turnstiles and ticket inspectors, and installed fake mirrors and dim blue lights in the toilets. They'd replaced the soft incandescents with fluorescents. But still, post-renovations, it remained a good place to meet boys. Lots of young travellers milling.

One time I met a beautiful African with lips that started at my mouth and from there covered my entire body in soft, fleshy waves. He told me that I had a beautiful arse, shaped just like an African woman's. I flicked the tiny corkscrew of hair on the tip of his chin. 'You came all this way for some African arse?'

He had chocolate friends who melted away, and we ended up in his bed at the hostel. Everything was going fine under threadbare, apricot-coloured sheets. My jeans were off, his jeans were off but then he wouldn't let me put his dick between my legs. He pulled back, he twisted, he bent. 'What's up, Slippery?' I asked. He looked at me and blinked his slow, black almonds. 'What do you mean?' he asked. 'What do you mean, what do I mean?' I asked. We lay there breathing. His cock in my hand was hot and hard. He gently brushed a strand of hair out of my eyes. 'I want to wait,' he said. 'Wait for what?' I asked. He looked at me with his black impenetrables. 'Until I'm married.' He came closer, breath on my cheek. I let go of his dick and pushed him away. 'Oh, for Christ's sake.' I tore back the crappy sheets, pulled on my jeans and stomped out to the sound of him wheedling, 'Wait, wait, come on! We can do other stuff!'

I didn't have time to negotiate. He seemed nice, and was a legendary kisser, but I didn't have time to fuck around.

Oh My Godfather

Barriers like Africa arose from unexpected quarters. Sometimes religious. Sometimes anatomical. I discovered that dicks could be clumsy, unpredictable fuckers.

That summer, Eddie's cousin Gavino came over from Malta. He wore Aviator sunglasses and gelled his hair; told story after story, his English spastic with upward inflection. He said that if all the expat Maltese went back to Malta at the same time, the island would sink. He smoked from the side of his mouth, keeping the cigarette clamped on one side of his lips, exhaling and talking through the other side.

We went to the movies and saw *The Godfather: Part II*. Eddie on one side, Gavino on the other, me getting sprinkled with popcorn. We fell out onto the street and Gavino's accent swung towards America. He told me they had dynasties in Malta; that he was part of one. He told me, through the crack in the right-hand side of his lips, that in Malta no one fucked with him. 'Well,' I said, 'you're not in Malta now.' Eddie snorted. Throughout my adolescence I found misunderstandings like these to be frequent occurrences.

Anyway, it went like this: Eddie's at work, Mum's at work, and me and Gavino are in my bed, my blackout blinds doing their job, and nothing I try will work, and then Gavino's weeping and yanking at himself, increasingly violent. 'Not now,' he's moaning. '*Not NOW.*' I'm rolling my eyes at the ceiling and he's screaming and swearing at his poor, uncooperative cock: soft and warm and pliable as a raw sausage left out in the sun.

Turns out, I would've been his first. Turns out, the other Godfathers would've been envious as all hell.

Four, Five and Six

Four, Five and Six — apart from their New Zealandness, Germanness and Greekness — were pretty much indistinguishable. I lost sight of my plan that year. I was smoking a lot of Eddie's neighbour's crop and if it wasn't for my Moleskine I may have forgotten them. Boys of this age . . . it was generally all over lickety-split; in, out, who'd remember? And I'd entered a time of no memory, a slowly unfurling ever-present. Thank God for my journal, or what a waste, even without distinguishing details. So numbers Four, Five and Six were destined to remain merely numerical.

Stephen

Except that there was a future at the tip of these unfurling moments: University. I re-remembered its name in Year Twelve. By then I had a reputation as school expert, though I'd neither confirmed nor denied a thing.

My mother once told me not to do or say anything I wouldn't be happy to do or say in front of her. I snorted when she said it and she slapped me hard. I understood that she had to be tough – that she couldn't pull the 'just wait till your father gets home' number. I thought about what she said, and how funny it was that there were things I did that I would die if certain people found out about, and – at the same time, for the same things – that I would die to let other people know. I thought this was a psychological conundrum; thus my interest in Psychology.

One lunch I found myself telling all this to Stephen, even though I'd never really spoken to him before. Even though I'd never really *seen* him before. Stephen was Australian by birth, and in the other Year Twelve class. He wanted to study Geography or Anatomy. He said they were both about the exploration of new territories. I called him Christopher Columbus and we laughed. All of this surprised me.

'I'm hardly Columbus,' he said shyly, and then told me he was nineteen years old, which is old for Year Twelve, and this fact was compounded by the other fact: he was a virgin. He felt this was holding him back with women; he felt he couldn't face a uni chick as a virgin.

So. Although I'd already covered Australia, and Stephen was a geek, I offered to help him out. He said, 'Wow' a few times, his eyes a bit bulgy, and then he raved on and on about women and love and *making love* and being old already, and I had to try and remember not to roll my eyes, or to sigh. *I've agreed already*, I wanted to yell at him and shake him by his curly, whitish hair, and push his eyeballs back where they belonged, inside their sockets, but in the end I just nodded and half smiled, and felt a bit sorry for him.

Flat

We meet one Saturday lunchtime at his brother's flat; the brother being away for the weekend. It's a one-room-holds-it-all kind of flat – kitchen, lounge room, dining room and bedroom, all tumbled on top of each other like different shoes shoved into one box. A sliding door marks a tiny, side-box bathroom. Stephen has lit about a million candles and sticks of sweet incense. A woman is screaming in opera. There's an actual bottle of champagne sweating on the kitchen bench. *Jesus Christ*, I want to say, but study the photos on the fridge instead. Stephen's crouched over the CD player, fucking with the volume. In the photos there's this one guy with dead-straight brown hair – sometimes in his eyes, sometimes slick – holding up a variety of beers with his arm around a variety of girls, mostly blondes with unfocused eyes. 'He's studying law,' Stephen says.

He's still crouched by the stereo, but he's looking at me, guiltily, like it's all his fault that his brother has a hundred and fifty drunk girlfriends. He straightens up and brushes his hands on his jeans, as if he's just built the fucking CD player from scratch. I watch him, suddenly curious, as if the world has just shrunk down to him and me. He clears his throat. 'So,' he says, 'would you like a drink?' The word *drink* a tremble. I tilt my head to one side, watching Stephen the white-haired boy from school. His cheeks are flushed dark pink and his eyes are wetter and wider and far, far darker than usual. 'Don't be scared,' I say, and then take his hand.

Stephen kisses me as if he's afraid he might bruise my lips. He kisses me so soft I could cry. His eyelashes are white feathers against his cheek. He lifts my T-shirt over my head and he's caressing me with his soft fingertips and whispering lips. Even those lashes are playing with my skin. The candles toss slow shadows; the chick cries sad opera. And then we're on his brother's bed and somehow his tongue is between my legs and doing what my finger normally does, where my finger normally does it. And then it's me who's trembling and trembling and I start to forget who I am, where I am, my plans, my plans to give plans, and he's making my body do things I didn't tell it to, things I didn't tell him to do, and so I kick Stephen off me and go, 'No. Not like *that*. Like *this*,' and I jump on him and viciously shove his cock inside me, and flinching, I make sure it's over for him in a few seconds – he makes a little grunt – and then I get off and throw my clothes on, not even bothering to wipe myself, and he's sitting up looking sort of stunned and slack-jawed, and I can't meet his eyes, I can't.

'Okay,' I say. 'There you have it. Not so difficult. See you round.'

He says nothing. Then he says, 'What?' That one word, confused and hurt.

I'm at the door, looking at my hand on the deadlock. I want to scream that *I don't know what. How the fuck would I know what?* I want to scream it, but I start crying. And again, the softest lips in the world carve that confused and hurt word – 'What?' – out of my air.

Skin

I run to the station after another sleepless night, cursing time: more when I want less, none when I need more. I jam the hands of an imaginary clock and feel them slice through my fingers.

By the time I step into the bland hum of the air-conditioned train and catch my reflection in the window, the flexures of my elbows are burning. I sit and scratch my arms, one at a time, then together. I dig at the moist skin, stripping the top layer, scratching for relief but only making the itch worse. I have suffered this inflammation since I was a girl. It's my symphony, my bull ant serenade. My mother took me to the local doctor once, and thereafter to naturopaths, herbalists, homeopaths. She put me on diets. She rubbed my skin with the benign and the hideous: crushed juniper berries, chamomile tea and one time, a tar-based sheep-dip.

One of the therapists finally concluded, 'It's her nerves.'

And after that, when I would scratch, my mother – then into ceramic painting, and dressing in immense kaftans – would bring her face in too close and tell me to calm down, to take long, slow breaths. Even in public – at book launches with poets reciting in aggressive intonations, around tables crowded with cranks. Her voice, crashing with importance and cheap red, 'Come on, Georgie, *breathe* with me.'

The train heaves itself along. I scratch until my nails are full. We pull into the station near the university and I assess my bare arms. Disappointment descends. Outside, the sun screams. I hide my reluctant limbs inside my heavy brocade jacket. I pick up my bag, and I wince.

The classroom is bald under white fluorescent tubes. I choose a seat as far away from the other students as possible, keep my eyes on the dark crevices in my knuckles, sit tight in my heat. The others chat, stretch out, hang arms over chairs; a woman nearby lifts handfuls of auburn hair and twists it up off her neck. I watch the miraculous skin from the corner of my eyes and can taste bitter almond and milk. Rachel enters wearing beige silk. Her hair is Japanese black. We are all in love with her, and read her novels for clues. She looks around the room, greets us with perfect, coral-coloured lips, and suddenly there are clouds of something Cacharel.

In this class we read Freudian case studies as literary documents, and I am every patient I read: Wolf-man, Rat-man, Dora. These aren't literary documents, they are caves of existence that I mine for answers about myself. Last week we read that the Wolf-man – like me – clamped his teeth together and used them to filter his saliva: a way of keeping things outside a far too permeable skin. Today we discuss Dora's body and I imagine her wearing the one corseted dress, day after day; how lovely, how simple. The tight bodice, the layers of cool fabric swishing around your ankles and hips, like waves. I imagine looking up at old man Freud.

A male student with dark hair and a faded orange T-shirt slides into the seat next to me. I pin my arms to my sides and my jacket's lining welds to my sweaty, stinging skin. I keep my breaths small, pull in close to the table, so that it digs beneath my ribs, so nothing can get out. I feel him at my side, a sheer vertical mass.

Rachel says, 'George?' and I jump at my name. George: easy to give, not so easy to wear, but Eliot claimed it for women, you know. My name, so ugly; my mother's political accessory. 'What do you think?' Rachel's cool, direct gaze.

I give a taut smile. What do I think? I think I should have tied my hair back, should have pulled it from my face, sprayed perfume down my dress, worn a different dress, pants even, and deodorant. I want to go home and start again. What do I think? Just wishing I were Dora; in another century; in another outfit; in another skin. I raise a shoulder, shake my head.

Rachel turns to another student. 'Keith?'

Keith straightens his rectangular glasses, puts down his pen and puckers. 'Well . . . I think Dora triumphs over Freud's dominance through her severance of the treatment. In the end it is *she* who makes the cut.'

Someone sniffs. I think about a blood-draining cut, and the relief it could bring. A Victorian dress has so many layers; from the outside you could not even tell.

'Very good,' Rachel tells Keith, and we watch her coral lips bloom. 'An incisive analysis.'

I fill my bath with cool water. The scratch marks on my arms, behind my knees, on my thighs and my stomach all sing sharp and high when I lower myself in. I soak until my fingertips macerate white. Then I lie back on my bed, naked and wet, with the fan blowing over my nagging flesh. Saturday is Ruby's birthday party. I haven't seen her since she flew to America, to Duke University for her PhD.

We met in a first year philosophy lecture. The lecturer was one of those tall, thin, bent-over men who wear socks with their sandals all year round. In a fury – as usual – he arced his forefinger around the room. 'The fact that you all eat meat is based upon the premise of "might equals right". And if you lot ever *thought*, you might finally recognise your *neanderthal* barbarism.'

Ruby had taken to sitting next to me in the lecture theatre from the start of the year. She leaned over and whispered, 'Let's get the hell out of here, all this talk of meat has me hankering for a burger.' And although I liked to witness the lecturer's fury from the safety of the sleepy crowd, I was captured by her plans.

Ruby was plain, but when she walked into a room she expected everyone to look. She had that: high expectations. And everyone would look. They would watch because she demanded it; they would watch just to see what might happen. Or, at least I would watch her. I would watch Ruby.

We became friends. She was the only person I had ever known who could handle my mother; they were loud, opinionated and ironic in equal measure. When the three of us were together, I felt suspended between these two large people who took up all of the room, disparaging some radio announcer I'd never heard of, the governmental budget, a film, and chain-smoking hand-rolled cigarettes. I felt shielded by them: safe and small.

Ruby and I had kept up a sporadic email correspondence after she left for Duke. But what could I say?

What had I done? My weeks were deserts. Occasionally I would write an email full of lies: *Well, I haven't been able to decide yet between Shaun – you know, that young psycho-analyst – and Fred, the playwright.* My little ficto-lives I would write and then delete.

What could I say about this week? That I'd daydreamed about Dora. That I'd composed a few new outfits. That I'd itched and stung and scratched and burned.

I first knew of Ruby's return when I saw her picture in the weekend paper. Her knowing face nestled between two pretty others, six eyes squinting with laughter. They were in another universe, everything about them glossy. Ruby's hand gripped a tilted glass of champagne.

I really needed fame. That would make it easier. Perhaps I could write a fake memoir. Some ribald tell-all about a childhood of enforced bestiality. My mother made me and she filmed me and they hurt me. *Girl Who Got Fucked By The Wolves*. Now that would bring me fame.

Ruby called a week later, exuberant phrases burning my ear.

'Of course I'll come to your party,' I said.

What to wear to Ruby's party? I study her picture. I need sleek black clothes, dark lips, some glitter about the ears. I need sharp, shiny hair. I need happiness and success. I start from naked; face my open wardrobe. Surely every combination hadn't been exhausted. Some-times your wardrobe can surprise you. Sometimes you can find yourself dressed as someone unexpected. Grandma's brooch, plus Zambesi singlet. Pencil skirt over tights under boots. I look in the mirror, stick my left hip forward, cup my shoulders. It's not quite there. Coco Chanel said, 'Before you leave the house, look in the mirror and remove one item.' I peel off the top, stare at my breasts sitting eager above all of that irritated, flaky skin. Could I pin the brooch through my nipple? The blood would be referential fringe-eighties, very of-the-minute. I put my hands on my hips and bass flute, 'And here we have George, dressed exclusively by Eczema.' I slink back to the cupboard. I need something wrist to neck to ankle; this skin is not party skin.

I wake and pull my hair back into a tight ponytail. I have my first appointment with the hairdresser in two years. I chose the salon from a magazine the night Ruby called. The Alley Vee: multi-award winning cutters, stylists, colourists, technicians. Highlights, lowlights, bio-ionic straightening.

I try long sleeveless dress over short boots. I try belted man's shirt with tuxedo pants. I try the man's shirt under tunic with knee-length boots. Then I pull on the pencil skirt, tights and singlet from last night, and cover my arms with my jacket.

I push through an immense glass door with a jagged iron, A-shaped handle, and walk into a club reeking of burnt hair. People scream and squeal in each other's ears, poke sharp tongues, splay sharp fingers. Everyone's hair looks like origami. As the apprentices strut the floor, they turn and watch their own hot arses ignite the mirrors.

My jacket is taken by stealth. I snap my red arms across my chest and stand folded, until I'm wrapped in a black gown and pushed onto a scoop of leather. Now I am salon client, just a head above a cape: anonymous.

Oh mirror, mirror, what do I see? Sunken eyes, acne scars and a ponytail of split ends. My adrenaline heart meets the rhythm of the music. There's a lot riding on this haircut, Ruby.

A fat girl with black and red hair and a surly face walks towards me. Please, why can't I have that one over there who looks like my high-school art teacher? Or her, the Chinese girl with a Mohawk? Why always the fat girls? I find it hard to breathe around them. They remind me of kaftans and whole tofu cheesecakes, of asphyxiating joss sticks and group hugs.

Monique introduces herself in a New Zealand monotone, around a great wad of gum. She descends heavily onto a stool behind me, releases my hair, rifles through it and her bored look turns to appalled. Her bubblegum breath boogies my cheek, she holds out a short piece of my hair. 'Why are there chunks *missing* from your hair?'

'Relics of my desperation,' I whisper.

She drops the chunk and sighs. 'How short do you want it?'

'How short is life?' I answer.

She looks at me with her broad, blank face.

My sore skin and shiny new hair are strange bedfellows. I should write an essay: 'The incommensurable problematic of inflammation and coiffure: Image, annihilation and restoration; The female form, the market and the mirror image; Stylistics and self-destruction.' I could stretch the rope of sub-titles on forever, but then what would I do with it?

I'm polishing wine glasses at Claude-Michel's, the last customer gone. Claude-Michel is hunkered over his bowl of noodle and raw egg. I hear pots thrown against sinks, and the wet roar of the dishwasher. I gaze down at my long black apron. Perhaps I could go to the party as a waiter? *Oh my God! I thought it was fancy dress!* Perhaps I could actually *be* Ruby's waiter? *A drink, madame? An hors d'oeuvre? No? Please. I insist.*

'Big date tonight, daydream-Georgie?' Claude-Michel asks with his mouth full.

'I don't know any men, C-M, only academics.'

'Eh?' he says and spoons in another mouthful of noodle, his jaw working like crazy. 'I am a man, no?'

'Yes,' I say, and lift a tray of glasses. 'An old man.'

I always smile when he snorts.

I love this job. Strapped in tight, in my starched apron and my long-sleeved crisp, black shirt. I am George The Waiter, diplomatic mediator between the customer and the kitchen; repository and fulfiller of other people's desires.

Listen, C-M, cook their fucking steak well done or I walk.

I remember how customers like their coffee, even if they don't come back for months. *Extra strong short macchiato, wasn't it? Decaf skim cappuccino?* I remember favourite tables, favourite wines. I remember who ordered what and how. I am so good at this job I should be a franchise: Oh-How-Georgie-Can-Wait.

I set the tray of glasses down on the table behind Claude-Michel. He slurps red wine. He says, 'We could go to a bar, yes? Why not? I mean, we are both free tonight, and 'ere, together, no?'

I stop mid-twist. 'What?' I look down at his hair. Metallic flecks glint like fool's gold through the black. He turns and looks up at me with his blue pebble eyes. I see, in that moment, my skin in my mirror: my crimson clouds, my rough, red skin. His eyes have that need, that generic, neon want. Nothing to do with me.

'Sure, C-M, free and *ear*. We could go out listening!'

'I am serious,' he says. 'We will 'ave fun.'

'Fun,' I say and wonder at the word while the dish-cloth drags my fingertips.

I procrastinate home over cigarette butts and bottle tops; so much urban confetti. How will Ruby see me? Blind worming through a degree. Still an undergraduate. Undergraduating. Undergraduated. Crawling as she soars.

There is blood on my sheets when I wake up. Constellations. Red dwarfs. My nails are full of dried blood. Behind my knees, in the crook of my elbows, down my forearms, between my breasts, my skin lives. It cuts and spins for me, like a sadistic DJ offering vicious, throbbing songs.

I stand, catch sight of myself in the wardrobe mirror:

I've been massaged with acid, stripped and burned. I sit on the floor in front of my wardrobe, unsure of what to do. If I call my mother, she'll talk to me like I'm a mental patient. 'Now, Georgie, you know what to do. Breathe, just *breeeathhhe.*'

I scream into the mirror, 'I *am* breathing, you fat old cow, I *am* breathing. Do I look like I'm holding my breath? Do I look all blue?' I sit and watch myself pant. I am belted with a tornado of desire to cause violence and pain. And I know I will direct it to myself. I look away from my pandemonius skin and whimper. I must do something, anything, before I reach muscle and bone. I have an appearance to make, an important appearance, and I need to get real help.

I open the Yellow Pages to 'D' for dermatologist. How obvious, how plain to see – once the idea dared to enter my mind – that for a *skin problem* you should see a *skin doctor.* Who gives a damn if the rash is a symptom of something *deep.* I'm done with deep; who the hell has time for deep? What's wrong with a bit of only-treating-the-symptom when time's not on your side?

I call the only female. I need something to differen-tiate the list of names; their inconsequential choice of font, their suburban geography. May as well divide them down sex lines. Dr Linda Kempson, and there has been a cancellation, so I can come at 3 pm, otherwise I can come in four months. I pause when the receptionist tells me this – I am silent for a stupidly long time – and she makes an impatient, you-are-obviously-an-idiot kind of sound that I am unable to bear and so I blurt out, 'Yes, 3 pm, I can make it.'

I exhume a loose white shirt, and a long grey skirt that almost hides my boots. I split the outfit at the waist with a thick leather belt, then I stand back and appraise. Ruby would twist her earring, twist her hair, twist her scarf, shake her head like I'm a hopeless case and then tell me I look like a bank clerk.

The bus lets me out amongst old-fashioned roses, fat bees and pretty fences with numbers in brass. I'm the only person on the footpath. Occasionally a car hums by. I try not to stare at the shaded, heritage windows, for someone may call the police.

And who are you, miss?

Who am I? Goodness, I haven't the faintest idea! I'm just a dermatological case in search of a miracle. I'm just a girl in a long grey skirt. My mother's daughter. Admirer of Ruby.

Dr Kempson's rooms nestle in a cul-de-sac off an elm-lined street. A sleek, silver Audi rests in the driveway. Five patient car spaces hold sparkling new cars.

I fill in a form for the receptionist and wait on a suede couch. I don't look at the other patients; what we are engaged in here is as private as a gasp in sleep – our skins. I stare down at my boots against the high shine of the floorboards. I never think about polishing them until it's too late.

Dr Linda Kempson's skin has no pores. She is perhaps fifty with short, silver hair and pale blue eyes. She wears layers of fine cloth in shades of ivory. She tilts her porcelain head when I tell her that my skin hurts. She examines my fingers between her cool, soft hands. I notice, for the first time, my dirty nails. Dr Kempson asks me to take off my clothes and lie on the table. The room smells of disinfectant. I concentrate on a tiny gap between the floor and the wall as I undress and lie on the starched cotton like a foetus in underwear, trying to fold back inside. Dr Kempson wears gloves the colour of Elizabethan skin. She starts the unfolding at my arms; positions the steel limb of a halogen lamp above what she wants to see. She touches and strokes and moves with her light. I turn and shift and unbend at her bidding. I'm dreaming of outfits. Can't afford Akira? You can always shred an old kimono found in the back of a junk shop. Belt it the right way, over footless black tights and you'll have an approximation. Prada? Dye neat frocks black, and carry a big beige purse. Philosophy by Alberta Ferretti? Bruised eyes, no lips, and cute little black ribbons tied tight around your neck. With a bit of work and a handful of coins, you can come to resemble almost anyone.

'Okay,' she tells me, 'you can get dressed now.'

I pull on my clothes, buckle my belt one notch too tight and sit on the edge of a chair. She washes and dries her hands. She has not yet smiled. I watch her and imagine my dirty fingers gripping her porcelain jaw until she opens her pink mouth to let out a cry. I see my violet fingerprints all over her skin. I feel as if we've just fucked, and it was totally against her wishes. *Georgie-Porgie pudding and pie kissed the girls and made them cry*. I look down and press my rough hands together in guilty prayer.

Dr Kempson glides into her chair. 'George, you have dermatitis of a particular variety; you have what is called "atopic dermatitis". You are "atopic".' She pauses, for my digestion.

'Atopic?' I say. 'Without topic?' I always suspected that was my problem: my complete lack of a topic.

A smile threatens the edge of her cool. 'Atopic means allergic.'

'Yes.' I can't help the sigh. 'I know.'

Thursday and Friday: I lie in my apartment, using Kempson's creams, thinking of her delicious frost and watching my skin turn from angry to blush. *She kissed the girls and made them cry.* I eat only liquids. I move only slowly. I am desperate to feel comfortable in my own skin. The beautiful doctor couldn't tell what I'm allergic to, but apparently with creams like these it doesn't matter. I read a month of glossy magazines and study the society photographs. I read articles about cut-rate plastic surgery, about women who kill their children. I read about husbands who cross-dress, and how to give them mind-blowing head. I read about the phenomenon of synaesthesia, where colours have a smell, and sensation has a sound. I figure I am synaesthesic: sensation has a colour, desire has a sound, and they've been screaming red for years.

On Saturday morning I open my wardrobe and coach myself and my clothes: *Deconstruct! Reverse the natural order! Turn singlets inside out and back-to-front. Layer dress upon dress upon dress. Wear petticoats on top of your jeans, belts around your head. Thread all of your jewels on a single chain and wear it as a G-string.*

Act like a sentence: let your clothes speak a thousand words; drape your bones in poems.

I'm an atopic subject snatching, losing grip on her verb. A girl named as a boy so her mother could be cool, with no adjective to contain me, besides some terribly fucked up skin. I wait for evening. On my bed, a pillow crushed into my stomach, I push aside the magazines and read Freud's essay, 'Mourning and Melancholia'. The difference between mourning and melancholia, Freud writes, lies in what is empty: your world or your self. Pretty pictures rise and float in my mind: noise and action frozen, from some magazine, from some place else. I look at the outfit I've chosen, lying in wait across the chair. What is it about Ruby, after all? I see two little girls, face to face, playing hand-clap games. They chant: *'Scratch and win. Swap your skin. Scratch and win. Swap your skin.'*

Ruby, she fills my world, she fills my self. I stare at my outfit and I wait. Then I get up to go to her party – George, and a pile of clothes – and the skin beneath my sleeves sings her a song.

Poetics of Space

. . . we construct the world – an enormous nest,
an agglomerate of earth and sky, of death and life,
and of two sorts of time, one we can dispose of and
one that is lacking.

– Boris Pasternak

I reasoned it thus: you have eight weeks to write your entire honours thesis on *The Poetics of Space*. Retreating is easy. Dead easy. Turn the backseat of your 1978 Celica into a strewn bricolage of your belongings: threadbare tuxedo pants, four-dollar cleanskins, three trashy novels, your vintage laptop and printer, a new ream of recycled A4. Stash contraband in the boot: sixty-eight library books you couldn't open at home. Too noisy, too late, too early. Too noisy. Say a prayer: *Great Aunty Hilda, thank you for dying and leaving a wooden shack in sixty acres of gum that the family was forbidden to sell for 110 years.* When I asked if I could stay, they said I could burn the place down.

I turned off the Hume Highway and followed a map my dad had sketched for me on a flimsy pink napkin. On the back he had drawn tense instructions for firing the generator. He thought I was mad. 'It's just barren land,' he kept telling me.

I reasoned it thus: you cannot procrastinate in the bush. You cannot have writer's block. You cannot spend your days ignoring the faults of a very boring boy called Phil Gerard. You cannot spend your days at Hoyts or Lumière cinemas with your face ghost-lit and the rest of you lost. You cannot lose days along laneways prickling with edgy boutiques, streets black and dense with groove, or at a pinch David Jones, smearing tester after tester onto the back of your hand. Like palmistry on the reverse side, searching for perfect red, you tilt your hand and see all the different shades in all the different lights. In the bush, I reasoned, you cannot spend days lost.

I arrived at the local town. Everybody there smoked: skinny women, fat men, girls so young they wouldn't have a clue how far they'd come. There was a caravan park families lived in all year round. Old men shuffled the street wearing poo-coloured cardigans. Old ladies followed them with pencilled-on eyebrows. The youths all had concertina limbs they opened and closed, opened and closed. Those in between – the ones stretching their kids' arms – looked pinched and mean. In the tiny supermarket I bought spaghetti, canned tomatoes, six tins of minestrone. I bought bread, milk, chewing gum, and Coco Pops for dessert.

It was 50 kilometres from the town to Hilda's. Her shack – a wretched little box all dressed up like a log cabin – looked like senile dementia. Treated pine logs drooped. The paint around the aluminium windows had fallen away in clumps, like caking metallic eye shadow. A porch encircled the entire structure like a rusty walking frame. Trees and grass struggled against death. The air was thin and it was cold.

'Well,' I said out loud, 'I wouldn't call it *barren*.' I said the word over and over as I lugged my gear inside: *Barren. Barren. Barren.* I said it so many times the word began to sound like an ancient battle, like a woman's name, or like a nonsensical collection of syllables I had inadvertently coined and now couldn't get rid of.

I dragged the kitchen table in front of the window overlooking the porch and piled my books on either side. Every movement I made sounded huge. I stacked tinned minestrone in the pantry, next to Hilda's bran. I worked out how to power the generator, heat the water, use the radiator and gas stove. In Hilda's bedroom I discovered a perishing hot water bottle and a cupboard full of crocheted blankets. The delicate smell of baby powder clung to everything in the room. I counted months and marvelled at the scent's tenacity. Then I slouched in front of my laptop. Out of the window I could see the topmost railings on the porch. I could see dirt, trees, the driveway, my yellow Celica. On my right: piles of books. On my left: piles of books. I worked on my thesis: THE POETICS OF SPACE. I worked on it: *the poetics of space*. I worked on it: *THE POETICS OF SPACE*. I thought about tea. Then my brother drove in the gate and parked his burgundy ute beside my car.

He said, 'I heard there was some work near town.'

He lit a cigarette. I cleared my throat. We went inside, him all the time surveying, surveying. Edges, surfaces, little shady spaces, promising lumps in the linoleum. Hearing about work was his job. In my head words did battle with words: parasite versus history. But she was Aunty to us both.

His eyes on my desk, my books, my computer. 'I swear I won't get in your way.'

'Fine,' I said and slammed the homemade screen door.

Kevin drove all the way to town and brought back fish and chips for dinner. Potato and oil reeked strong and universal, like something salty gestating in damp paper, something barely kept under wraps. We sat side by side on the sunken couch. He opened the package on top of Hilda's fancy coffee table – probably the last of the family heirlooms.

'Can't you make your own pool of sauce?' I asked.

Kevin ate cold chips. I poured wine into coffee cups. We stared at the wall in front of us.

Kevin said, 'Remember sneaking over to Darren's to watch *Prisoner*?'

We stared at the wall.

I said, 'The sets were so small. As if it was filmed in a lounge room.'

'Rooms *are* small in prison.'

I shrugged.

Kevin lit up. 'And remember how you cried when they played the theme song.'

I drank wine. Kev smoked.

'Soap opera,' I said.

I woke, made tea and crouched in front of the radiator. Kevin had already gone. I crawled to the desk, typed *Chapter One*, deleted that, typed *Introduction*. I felt something in my belly. Hunger. Panic. My liver. Who knew? I thought I should eat. I huddled next to the radiator eating burnt toast with blue fingers. Breakfast over, I selected a book. The one put out by the groovy publisher, edited by a Mafioso. I took to Hilda's bed and buried myself under her five multi-coloured, crocheted blankets. The book creaked. I scanned the index. I woke to the slam of Kevin's ute door.

That night we ate tinned soup and drank again from my pauper's cellar. Kevin had been hired to work at a chicken farm halfway between Hilda's and town.

Our eyes were on our bowls.

'So,' I said between mouthfuls I was trying to silence, 'are we talking cages, sheds or fields? Are we talking free-range, Omega-three or organic? What are they farming? Meat or eggs?' I looked at my brother.

Kevin stopped slurping, tilted his head to one side. 'Dunno.'

'How can you get a job if you don't even know what the job is?'

He looked down and slurped, 'I'm on Farm Number Three and I start at eight.'

His chin dribbled minestrone.

The next day my progress continued to thrill. Kevin arrived in the afternoon. His hair was wet. He said they had to shower before and after work in case they carried viruses. I asked him if they were positive that water killed viruses. He shrugged. I tried to keep my distance.

Kevin sat down. 'I had to sign a form promising not to take any chicken product either into or out of the farm. I had to agree not to have any type of bird or pig as a pet. Don't ask me what it is about the pigs, though, and then I had to help landfill nine hundred undersized roosters.'

Kevin laughed at the look on my face. 'Welcome to the real world, brains.'

By the end of the week I was doing aerobics to my own version of 'He Used to Give Me Roses'. Plans came and went like stunted roosters being pushed into holes.

Kev came home from work each afternoon talking like amphetamines.

'My job,' he said, 'is mostly to dole out the food. Now. You might think that is simple, or unimportant or something. But Joe, the other feeder, he accidentally dropped a bucket of food pellets in the middle of a shed. And. Well. First he had to run for his life and then we just had to stand back and watch as the chickens went sick, man. Eighty-seven chickens were suffocated. And,' he held up his forefinger like this was theology, 'it was all the ones that got there first.'

I drank my wine.

Kevin continued. 'And. Get this. A fox got into the shed on the weekend and ate two chickens.'

He looked at me.

I sighed.

He looked at me.

'And? So?'

'Man-oh-man! We lost *six thousand* chickens because they all charged away from the fox to this one end of the shed and were crushed to death.' Wild gesticulation was no longer beyond him. 'It's like there's these chickens, man, and they can't help but run and because there is no place to run they all *die*.'

'Kevin,' I said. 'You're sweating over Hilda's couch.'

He looked down at his thighs, his arms caught in kung-fu. He looked at me and his arms continued, 'They try to get away and just get fucken *crushed* in the process. It's like, "Don't run, man, there's no place to run. Just be cool, why should the fox pick you?"'

I drained my glass. 'What about letting the chickens live outside?'

He gripped the sides of his wet head. 'They still pulverise themselves! Against the fucken *fences*!'

'Oh.'

'Fences, walls, tractors, a pile of sticks! *A pile of sticks!*'

'Fine.'

'They find *something* to crush up against – no paddock can go on forever.' The forefinger was up.

'Fine, Kevin.'

'There is always some boundary –' the forefinger '– there was a mass drowning on Farm Two last year. Free rangers, bordered on one side by a creek. It was probably foxes again, but no one knows for sure.'

'Kevin.'

'Yes?'

'Please.'

'What?'

I got up.

'What?'

I slammed Hilda's bedroom door.

I took to Hilda's bed almost full-time. The merest glimpse of sunlight had me panicking. I couldn't avoid Kevin totally. He brought me my supplies. He told me stories, backlit from the doorway, about lard bins and rotting graves and spurting slit throats and maggots and thousands of dead little chicks. 'How's your work going?' he'd ask me with fear in his eyes.

I measured my days in Coco Pops and wine. Another box. Another bottle. Not a single lucid thought on the poetics of space. One morning I heard a noise from the porch and realised there were five bottles between me and the last time I'd felt the outside air. I opened the screen door. Something brown and white scurried under the bench seat. I crouched down and took a closer look. Beady eyes met mine, dead on. It was a baby magpie. '*Crawk*,' it said, tilting its head to one side.

'*Crawk* to you, too,' I muttered and stomped inside to close the blinds.

Now that I'd heard it, the magpie drove me nuts. I really needed silence. I'd come all this way for silence. I opened the door. 'What?' I yelled through the screen. 'What? What?'

Crawk was the answer.

'Who taught you to talk, Bird? Aren't you supposed to warble?' I set out a saucer of water, a piece of toast and counted silent minutes. One hundred and seventy passed before *Crawk* and a scratch at the screen door. I opened the door a crack and threw out a handful of Coco Pops. Then I sat in the lounge room counting minutes. Kevin came home.

'There's a baby magpie on the porch,' he said.

'Shhh,' I said.

'What? Are you okay?'

'The bird. *Crawk, crawk, crawk.*'

'You want me to kill it? I could kill it no probs.' He scratched his wet hair. 'I don't think I should have birds hanging around, anyway.'

'It's a magpie, Kevin. It's wild.' We looked at the screen door. The bird looked back at us.

We chewed spaghetti. We drank wine. We stared at the ·

wall. I was still in my pyjamas. I listened to Kevin suck spaghetti. I listened to the bird scratch.

Kevin said, 'We could park your car by the window and turn on the radio.'

I said, 'My radio's busted.'

'Oh,' Kevin said. 'So's mine.'

We stared at the wall and ate spaghetti.

I woke up under Hilda's blankets, sweaty and gasping. It was early, too early and I had neglected to draw the blinds. Under the rippling aluminium of the window frame I watched a trekking colony of ants. I wanted to run my finger over them in a gesture of smooth decimation. I would scream as I did it. Kevin and I had an ants' nest once; a slice of dirt pressed between sheets of clear perspex. The ants had made channels and tunnels and graves, and filled caves with their blind pupae. They had made spaces bloom in dirt. I heard a scratching at the screen door. I sat up and shrieked, 'What do you want from me? What?'

I got up, wrapped myself in a blanket and threw open the front door. Bird walked in like it was acting for Disney. 'Do come in,' I said as it made for the kitchen. I followed it and turned on the kettle. Bird gazed from me to the sink, hope illuminating beady, black eyes. I sighed and poured us each a bowl of Coco Pops. 'Know anything about the poetics of space?' I asked. *Crawk* was the answer. 'Thought as much.' We ate our breakfast. I shovelled. Bird ate pop by pop.

'So. Bird. You have a nest?' Bird looked at me and tilted its head. 'You know, a nest? With twigs and stuff?

Your home, the place you hang out, your space?' Bird tilted its head to the other side then made for a patch of sunlight on the linoleum. It sat down and rested its head on its chest. I watched it sit there. Bird watched me open a book. We listened to the spine creak large. I filled a page of A4. My notes approached lucidity. Bird sat quietly in its triangle of sunlight.

Kev came home with chips. My work was spread out on the table. Pages were filling fast. Bird stood by the couch.

'Just a minute,' I said, holding up my left palm. 'Just a minute.' I finished another sentence.

Kevin was smiling. The crooked smile he'd had since we were kids.

'Cool,' he said, eyebrowing my notes. 'Made friends?' he asked, nodding towards the bird. 'Food,' he said, holding up the chips.

We sat on the couch and he unwrapped our dinner.

'What's it about, anyways?' he asked around a mouthful of lukewarm chips. 'This paper you've been working on all year?'

'It's about space,' I said.

He looked at me. 'Like outer space?' His finger pointed up.

'No, like inner space.' I touched my fingers to my chest. I gestured around the room. 'Like inner space.'

We faced each other, my brother and I, on Hilda's sunken couch. And Bird sat between our feet, resting its head on its chest.

Shrink

My new friend's name is Sam. She is tall, a brunette and thirty-seven years old, like me. We meet for the first time over dinner at my old friend's house, where we discover we grew up five kilometres apart. We squint across the table trying to imagine childhood versions of each other.

'Oh my God!' we say, our voices suddenly nasal. 'Did you know Branco? That Spiteri went to jail? Do you remember the creek?'

'I know!' we both cry, in our childhood accents. 'I know! I know!'

My old friend says, 'Jennifer's a doctor,' and Sam's big grey eyes go wide.

She says, 'That's *amazing*. A doctor!' She says it over and over – *That's amazing! That's amazing!* – as if she cannot believe it, as if it is impossible, as if it is a miracle that our neighbourhood produced a doctor. Even though *she* emerged a lawyer.

We all drink a lot of wine and tell each other stories. I tell how I was thrown out of the local Blue Light Disco for getting drunk when I was twelve. How I went there searching for boys. Sam tells how she went to her law firm's fancy-dress party dressed as the Julia Roberts character from *Pretty Woman*. Our old friend laughs and says we both reckon we're Cinderellas. Then she tells us about her bastard ex-husbands as a warning.

As the dinner progresses, Sam starts peeling small strings of white flesh from the cold chicken carcass between us. Her broad shoulders curve in on themselves.

After dessert we all sit in a row on the couch and watch Woody Allen's *Interiors*. I have always loved

Woody Allen movies: good jazz tracks with contextu-
ally humorous titles, intricate conversation and complex
psychological motivation. I love how people in Woody
Allen movies say things you sometimes can't decipher
until afterwards.

It's because of Woody Allen movies that I always
wanted to be a psychiatrist.

I drive Sam home. We get into the car and our breaths are
big streams of white. Sam directs me through complex
twists and turns, through narrow hairpin bends, down
skinny streets, past rows of boxy weatherboard houses. I
am trying to talk to her and remember the number of
left turns we have taken.

She sighs and points with a limp hand, and I pull over.
She doesn't get out. She stares straight ahead at the boot
of an orange Corolla caught up in my headlights. Then
she stares out the side window, at her dark house. All
the houses in the street are crammed together, pressing
up against the footpath like a mouthful of bad teeth.
I wonder how I will find my way back home. I remember
my childhood street, our house sitting in its bare plot. It
feels as if Sam and I are long-lost sisters, reunited after
some perilous escape, and I wonder if we will ever see
each other again. The car's engine and heater hum.

'Do you remember the horses?' she asks and turns
towards me. She looks like a ghost under the streetlights.
A ghost with big soft lips.

'I remember,' I say. 'I wanted a grey horse more than
anything.'

'I had a horse,' says Sam. 'It was black. I rode it to the Laverton markets every Sunday.' She sighs and looks at her house again.

'What was its name?'

'What?' says Sam, as if I have distracted her from some complex observation.

'Your horse,' I say.

'Her name was Velvet.' Sam smiles and looks at her lap. 'Not very original, I know, but her coat did look exactly like velvet.'

'Don't worry,' I laugh. 'I was going to call my grey horse Storm.'

Before I meet Sam again I get married. We move to Sydney and I start my training in psychiatry. My husband Matthew is a doctor, too, in training to be a cardiologist. We have a running joke about our jobs: that we both look after people's hearts. His job, however, keeps him at the hospital, away from me, for more than ninety hours a week. Astonishing that I had believed a marriage ceremony would somehow fill a house.

I work in a huge psychiatric hospital full of secret police, messages from God, and people with CIA scanners in their ears. One patient sneezes herds of tiny purple elephants that chase her around the ward. There are patients who watch the floor and can't eat, who move through the hallways like dust. All the doors to the hospital are deadlocked. I have to carry keys and a personal alarm. I work exactly eight hours a day then go home to my quiet, empty house.

I visited a psychiatric hospital for the first time as a medical student. The consultant was a thin, elegantly-dressed man from India. He spoke a lot about Psychoanalysis. He spoke a lot about Buddha.

'Buddhism and Psychoanalysis,' he would say. 'Both teach us to coldly examine our desires. They teach us to set limits.'

And I would say, 'Hey! That reminds me of this Woody Allen movie where Woody decides not to start a doomed relationship with the twenty-year-old, even though he really, really wants to!'

The consultant said I was quirky. He had recently learned the word, and when he said it he would rock his head from side to side. He gave me one patient to look after by myself, under his supervision. The patient was a suicidal chef named Mark.

Mark was thirty-eight years old. He was tall with muscular thighs. His hair was cropped almost to the scalp. I would watch him talk. He kept his shoulders and his eyes pointing downwards, as if he wanted to slide right out of the world.

First he told me about his family in Ireland. Then he told me about his training in Paris. Then he told me about his cold ex-wife, his cold new apartment, the cold he woke up to in his bed at night. He spoke about the cold of silence. Then he told me, in intricate detail, how to cook canard confit, bouillabaisse, and mussels in white wine and cream. He taught me about Tarte Tatin, the apple pie that the Tatin sisters accidentally tipped upside down and found it was better that way. By that time there were not many silences. By that time we had taken to meeting in the corner of the courtyard where, just before lunch, a patch of yellow sun would appear for an hour. By that time I had noticed how blue his sad eyes were, how soft and dark pink and evenly creased were his lips. How you could, if you looked, make out the firm rise of his biceps beneath the cotton of his shirt. We would sit in the courtyard and I would listen and watch. Both of our stomachs would growl gently inside our clothes.

By that time his shoulders and his eyes were directed straight at me.

'Tarte Tatin,' Mark told me, 'is an apple pie that accidentally got spilled.'

'Tarte Tatin,' Mark said, his eyes inside mine, his tongue wetting his lips, 'is the quintessential example of a delicious mistake.'

Before I meet Sam again I visit my old friend in Melbourne. I haven't seen her for two years. We go to Carlton to see a re-run of Woody Allen's *Hannah and Her Sisters*. After the film we walk up Lygon Street. Despite the winter chill, the street is crowded with spaghetti-laden café tables and people licking gelati. Gleaming hot rods cruise. We walk into the quiet of Readings bookshop and take off our gloves. We are standing in front of the remainders table when my friend tells me that Sam and her boyfriend have broken up.

'Sam is suffering,' my friend says and flicks the pages of a novel. 'She thinks no one will love her, that she'll never find a husband, that she'll never have children, that she's no longer young, that there's no one left to find.' My friend flicks through the book. 'She's living on a mattress, on the floor, at my house.'

We go to Brunetti's. I push through the crowd and stand in front of the endless glass display case. Gorging on the hot smell of coffee, butter and ground almonds, I choose eight intricate biscuits; loneliness being some-thing I understand.

'This one,' I say and point, then walk the length of the display again while the girl serving me impatiently sucks in a cheek. 'And this one,' I say and point, in exactly the same way I used to point at the lollies kept in separate containers behind the glass at the Ardeer Milk Bar.

The girl puts the biscuits on a gold tray and wraps a sheet of clear cellophane around them. I hand them to my friend. I say, 'Tell her there are plenty to chose from. She does not have to be alone.'

I'm sitting at a tiny table on the balcony of a smoky bar in Melbourne. I'm drinking wine and staring out at the smooth, bud-lit branches of plane trees. I think about my husband Matthew, back in Sydney, at work. I think about the conference I've been trying to keep awake in all day, and my old dreams of psychodynamic-psychiatry, of psychoanalysis. Our med school psychiatry lectures were given by Rob – a charismatic man in his early forties, with a stylish wardrobe and frenetic gestures. I had no idea at the time, but Rob had never been a clinician. He'd received his medical degree and slipped immediately into an on-campus office, to study the history of medicine and of psychiatry, and to talk and talk and talk; not to patients, but to lecture halls filled with rapt students and burnt-out GPs. He spoke passionately of the old ways: of the talking cures, narrative, humanity, and free will. He was the med school's radical, proclaiming all that medicine had lost. We would meet for coffee and he would make the world sparkle, while I listened in keen adoration. And I know now what I did not know then: how easy it is to make the world shimmer and spark in your palm when you don't have the mess of a practice to filth it up; and that a single ordinary person, appearing before you at the right time with a sword of belief, can cut you a groove so deep you can't get out.

And today there were psychoanalyst-psychiatrists at the conference – not many, but some – sitting at the back in their superior silence; with their pointed noses and their steel spines. I was so sure I too would practise the old ways, until I saw that they had become priests. And now, I couldn't find my place. I'd walked into the conference and stood at the back of the hall, unsure of where I might sit, rooted by anxiety, desperately examining the back of the strange heads like a phrenologist.

Biology or religion, I'm tossing up between the two, while Tony Bennett croons the cool Melbourne air, and I am by myself as usual, but warm with red wine. I turn back to the crowd and there's a woman dressed in denim, with wavy black hair and smiling lips, her hand is on her hip and she's staring at my head. Then she's standing at my table and we're holding each other's shoulders going, 'No fucking way!'

When I first let on to Sam how much I liked Woody Allen she got a curve to her plump lips that flirted with becoming a scowl. I was describing *Crimes and Misdemeanours*, and I thought to myself when I saw Sam's expression, that she was lucky to have been born with a mouth that couldn't completely renege its promise.

'Woody Allen,' Sam said with her lips of contempt.

'No, listen,' I said. 'Wait. Two men are in love with the same woman. Woody Allen retreats so the producer, who fights, gets the woman . . . It's about willed action versus cowering. About taking a risk.'

'Men,' Sam said.

'The movie is full of ethical intricacies,' I argued.

Sam snorted.

'Just remember that comedy,' I quoted from the film, 'is only a tragedy plus time.'

Sam and I are sitting at the bar, slowly getting drunk. Sam says she keeps choosing men who don't want a serious relationship. She has theories about why she meets these kinds of men. She thinks it's because she's smart and men like women dumb. She thinks it's because she's forty and men like women under twenty-two. She thinks it's because she acts so tough even though she's vulnerable. She thinks it's her smart mouth, her politics, her nonnegotiable ideological positions. She thinks it's because of everything except her own intention.

Until I met Matthew, my relationships were complicated and exhausting, teetering and destructive. I knew Matthew wanted to be a Cardiologist and that he didn't much like children. I thought I knew what that meant. He had to ask me out four times before I said yes. I wonder now, was I nuts to flirt with disaster like that?

It is dark in the bar and the crowd walls us in with shoulders and backs, constructing a cubbyhouse privacy we would have had to make for ourselves as kids. Our eyes glint in candles; music twists our private air.

I tell her that maybe she should try doctors. 'Doctors,' I say, sparking and smiling and breathing heat everywhere, '*like* women who are smart and vulnerable.'

Sam looks at me, attentive.

'Believe me,' I say, swaying in, talking soft, 'a doctor would love you properly.'

Our skins are candle-light golden and we could be in a cave. I am overwhelmed at my happiness to be sitting somewhere not-alone; talking with a friend, about her, about me. It is intoxicating to be seen, to say a few words and be heard. I notice how close to her I have drawn, sit back, take a big swig of wine. Sam turns towards the bar, sighs. 'Where the hell am I going to meet doctors?'

Matthew has to work a month of nights. On Saturday and Sunday I creep around the house as he sleeps, picking up books and then losing interest. I sleep alone at night and have terrible nightmares: chainsawn lips, discarded careers, mangled husbands, babies gone blue. And me, trapped inside the Ardeer Milk Bar in a deserted paddock, unable to help anyone. I wake up alone with my hands on my belly.

In the psychiatric hospital we order a lot of pregnancy tests. When the manic girls start to get better, they slow down and start eating. Then they look down at their newly round bellies and think they are pregnant. They won't leave us alone until we test them. The tests are always negative, and when I tell them their tests are negative, the girls are always crushed.

I know I don't have forever, that by now I only have a couple of eggs left. But Matthew will no longer discuss it.

I meet Sam at the gallery. She has spent the weekend in Sydney with some guy. We go to see the Man Ray exhibition. She wears denim. I wear silk and lipstick. I have invited all of my male doctor acquaintances but only David turns up.

David is an Anaesthetist with curly black hair and implausible dimples. We've been friends since med school, and he never says no to me. He has strict, but ever-changing rules about what constitutes his type. Sometimes it's physique, sometimes it's education, sometimes it's creativity, sometimes it's nothing. His relationships never last long, but I haven't lost hope for him and he's the right age for Sam.

David and Sam take one look at each other and keep me between them like a wall. When David says something, Sam's eyes turn to flint and she yawns expansively. When Sam says something, the edge of David's mouth flips into an apostrophe and his right eyebrow moves up his forehead like a stretching cat.

We walk past walls of black and white photographs. I start to sweat and overcompensate. I chatter, I titter, I point.

Woody Allen, as you know, is a short Jewish man with many children. He has made over thirty movies and he acted in most of them, until old age exposed the inside of his bottom eyelids, as wet and pink as an internal organ.

In real life, Woody Allen has spent about a million hours on the couch with serial psychoanalysts, but he has never found relief. My bet is that when Woody Allen became famous his shrinks could no longer think straight. I bet they sat behind his head going, *I'm Woody Allen's psychoanalyst!* I bet they sat behind his head imagining themselves in his next movie. I bet they sat behind his head trying to make *themselves* into good characters.

In front of the long mirror in the gallery toilets, Sam tells me that the guy she's been seeing in Sydney is a nineteen-year-old guitarist from Norway who doesn't speak much English. I narrow my eyes slightly and pretend I'm checking my mascara.

She pulls at the sides of her un-made-up eyes. 'Why wouldn't I, Jennifer? It's not like I've got any better offers.' She picks the dry skin on her chin. 'Why wouldn't I?

I mean, what have I got to lose?' Her eyes slide across the glass to mine.

We plan to go back to my place, watch Woody Allen's *Celebrity* and eat dinner. I've seen *Celebrity* dozens of times. There are many characters:

> One always meets someone else right at the moment of happiness.
> One feels he has so much himself, that he can't refuse anybody a thing.
> One can't allow herself to have anything.

Sam, David and I go to the wharf market to buy fish to cook for dinner. The air is cold and wet and buoyant; an ocean of fish fillets glisten inside the glass cabinets.

David heads straight for the salmon. 'Hey, doc,' he says to me, and points at the chunks of salmon. 'Will you do that sashimi with the soy sauce and wasabi marinade?' Then he shows his wet teeth and makes his dimples go really deep. 'Please?'

'Salmon's endangered, David,' Sam says in a monotone.

David points at the sign. 'They're *farmed* salmon, Sam.'

Sam's eyes turn to stone. 'We shouldn't support the market for an endangered species. David.'

I look at my friends and feel responsible. I walk from one end of the cabinet to the other, cursing my impulse to matchmake. I peer at silvery scales, at blue and orange crustaceans, at freshly cut pink and white flesh. It's a goddamn coral reef suspended on ice and I am angry and sad. What's wrong with my friends? Why am I here, mediating between them, instead of next to my husband? Where the fuck *is* my husband; do I even have one?

I say, 'I've decided. I'll make mussels in white wine
and cream. I haven't made them for such a long time.'
I'm going to use the sad chef's recipe.

My new patient's name is Yolanda. She can't eat, she
can't sleep. Her face contorts with a terrible confusion
when she tells me she has nothing inside her. People
spend five minutes in a room with Yolanda and then
can't wait to get out. There's something asphyxiating
about her eyes. I work out a way of listening to her so
that I get a break now and then: I look at my notes, my
wedding ring, or my knees. The new ward consultant
is a young Psychiatrist with a deep love of ECT. He
speaks with Yolanda for a minute and a half and then
we leave. Back in the doctor's office, he says she needs
ECT.

'Electro-convulsive therapy?' I baulk.

'Yes,' he says, blank faced.

'Shock treatment?'

'Yes,' he says, blank faced.

'But we haven't even tried anything else.'

He hands me the second-opinion form necessary
to institute ECT. 'You have to sign this.' I tell him I
am sorry and stand there feeling torn. He blinks once,
deliberately, and hands the form and Yolanda's file to
Cindy, the other registrar. Cindy is round and vivacious.
She has a tiny mouth and big blue eyes. He doesn't need
to explain, Cindy smiles and nods agreeably.

'I'm sorry,' I say again to the indifferent air.

The consultant breezes out of the room without looking at me. Cindy giggles nervously. She wrinkles her nose and brings her little lips together. She says it doesn't matter that she's never met Yolanda, that she sort of knows the story and she'll read through the notes. She scribbles her neat little script on the form, saying over and over, 'ECT should be okay. It should be okay. It should.'

On Friday Yolanda said to me, 'The consultant told me if I want to get better, I have to *embrace* ECT. And I do, I do want to get better.'

I sat there and thought: *So, Psychiatry is about love, after all.*

David goes to buy the wine. Sam sits at the kitchen table while I scrub the mussels.

Sam says, 'It's impossible, Knut is too young.'

I scrub the beards from the salty black mussels just like the sad chef taught me. I wonder about him at times. Questions like: Does he have a family now?

Sam says, 'He only has his guitar and one bag of gear, he can get up and move on, in a second.' She clicks her fingers and then drums them on the table. 'Youth . . . the lightness of youth.'

Matthew is at work. I imagine him checking people's hearts, making sure they don't hurt, making sure they can get through the night. I imagine how relieved the patients must be to see him moving towards them through the dark. How relieved they must be to feel him.

Sam says, 'It won't last. What am I going to do? Quit my job and follow him around Europe on his gigs?'

I see a woman with golden-brown skin and a fat baby in an orange sling. She is smiling, walking barefoot, a man with a guitar by her side. It has been so long since Mathew touched me.

'Are you in love with him?' I ask.

'What's love?' she says. 'What the fuck is love?'

I wipe my hands on a tea towel and turn around to face her. 'It depends what you want.'

She looks around the kitchen. 'I want something solid . . . children. I really want children.'

'Children? He's nineteen, Sam! Why waste your time?' I splay my arms.

'I can just see it, Jennifer . . . I'm going to end up childless, alone.' Tears creep down her cheeks.

I imagine Sam and me, pressed up against the warm inside of our mothers' wombs, peering out through trans-lucent membranes to see what we're getting ourselves into. And our mothers move slowly through houses set in bare streets. They get them ready for us, their constant precious weights. An ache starts up deep in my belly. I always believed Matthew would change his mind. And I am so scared of the hatred in me that I see, but can't seem to feel.

Sam looks up. 'Maybe I should see a psychiatrist?'

My mouth shapes words without sounds. I am holding on so tight to my ferocious despair, no words can get out.

She whispers, 'I'm heavy with nothing.'

My cold hands grasp her wrists and hold on until I can breathe again.

The day they give Yolanda her first shock treatment I walk her to the ECT Suite. Neither of us says a word. The anaesthetist puts a tourniquet around her calf and injects her with a drug that paralyses her body and another that puts her to sleep. The ECT psychiatrist plasters electrodes all over her scalp.

He teaches me. 'We titrate the dose of electricity here . . . And this knob is where you dial up the dose.'

The anaesthetist puts on a Chemical Brothers CD. The nurse cracks a joke and everybody laughs. The psychiatrist flips the switch and I watch Yolanda's leg below the tourniquet start to shake. It jerks and convulses like a horrific frying sausage.

'Look,' says the psychiatrist, pointing at her foot. 'That's how we know we have the right dose. Enough to induce a grand mal seizure.'

'Look!' he says again, still pointing, as if her foot is a rare bird.

I watch her foot shake and imagine her soft, pink brain collecting its insults. The fitting goes on and on. The Chemical Brothers CD starts to skip: *Ro ro ro ro ro ro ro ro ro ro.*

The anaesthetist tells the nurse moodily, 'Move it to the next track, can't you?'

I am floating somewhere high above my body. 'Goodness,' I say to no one in particular, 'even the music is fitting.'

No one laughs.

I leave the ECT Suite and walk outside so I can breathe. The wind is fierce, trees shudder, flax plants convulse. I sit on a low stone fence and imagine a room full of patients wrapped head to toe in white cotton bandages; soft, dulling bandages. These people shuffle around an empty room, gently colliding, before floating away to bump into some other bandaged, muted person. I look down on these people, take a stirrer and spin it through the room. They are all caught up in the swirling wind and thrown into a hypnotic circle. They spin and spin until they start to homogenise into a dense white blur, until they liquefy into a wet mass that I pick up and drink. And my patients, they fill me, ameliorating my emptiness, soothing my hatred-burn.

We watch *Celebrity*. Kenneth Branagh has stuffed up *another* relationship. I point at the screen. 'You *see*?' I cry. 'He can't help himself. He wrecks *everything* he has.'

A few minutes later, Judy Davis gets cold feet on the day of her marriage to the perfect guy. I point at the screen. I cry, 'You *see*? She can't let herself *have anything*.'

I stand up and point at the screen. 'They return, they repeat, they are guilt-ridden and self-punishing. They *like* their symptoms, they *like* their suffering. They want it. They enjoy it. They *need* it! They need to destroy things, deny themselves, suffer.' I look from Sam to David. They are staring at me with their mouths slightly agape. I sit down and add calmly, 'It's the only explanation.'

David tousles my hair then leaves his fingers entwined. 'Jen, take it easy. It's just a film.'

'Don't be such a goddamn technician,' I say, conscious of the lovely, confusing presence of his hand in my hair. So long since I have been touched. 'Leave anaesthesia for a second here and think psychodynamically.'

'Hey,' he says, 'at least my job description's honest.'

'Is that right?' I jerk my head out from under his hand. 'I'll go fix dessert, then. Someone could come to the kitchen in a minute and help me carry.' I look at Sam but she is lost in the movie. Branagh has just left the perfect woman to be with Winona Ryder, who plays a sulky actress who is addicted to diet pills and infidelity.

'I'll come now,' says David, and gets up from the couch. 'I've seen this film a hundred times.'

I take a cake from the top of the fridge and put it on the table. David leans against the bench watching me.

I rip open a block of dark chocolate. 'What do you mean, it's not honest?'

'You know what I mean. I didn't mean to criticise *you*. You will be superb.'

I break the chocolate into a bowl, pour in cream, and put the bowl over a pot of water on the stove. 'Do you think we're eating too much cream?' I mumble.

'Jen, come on. You know . . . you know . . .'

'What I don't know is whether I can hack two more years of convulsion-therapy-prison-house psychiatry, of rendering people amnesic and anaesthetic in the name of fucking biologism.' I stir the chocolate. 'I thought my work would be like that film. I thought we would all sit around and discuss *why* people did things, *why* people felt things. I thought it would be about *helping*, not about banish-feelings-quick. I have been such a blind fool. But what am I supposed to do now? What else can I do?'

'I don't know, Jen.' He steps closer to the stove. 'But what I do know is that when I'm with you . . . I feel . . . happy.'

'What?'

David says, 'I said happy, I feel happy. Such a simple, rare thing . . .'

'Happy.' I turn to him.

'I can't hang around, Jen, it's becoming a sad joke. I'm going to join Médecins sans Frontières . . . go away. You could come with me. I need to ask you, to say it. We could go to Burma. Imagine Burma, Jen, with none of this empty crap.' David's arm points, his eyes search and my heart skips like a damaged CD. I focus on the beat. Matthew would have noticed my heart-beat, once upon a time. He used to say, *You've gone all tachycardic. You okay, Jen-Jen? You excited?* And the hatred is there again – that hard, mean stone – taunting me and complicating my life.

'I know you aren't happy, Jen.'

'What do you mean?' I touch my cheek. 'Why wouldn't I be happy? My job is a bitch at the moment, but that's not all I have.' My voice sounds shrill in my ears.

'We could have something. Please, let yourself. Let us.'

'Jennifer,' Sam yells from the lounge room, 'you need me to help?'

'I'm fine,' I call back, voice cracking like a plaster, and I turn away from David. 'Please, David, I need . . . I need time . . . I can't bear this.' I take a tea towel and lift the bowl of chocolate from the top of the pot. Steam rushes the room. I want to scream out in confusion and in fury: *What's happening here? I'm the one who knows what's what – me. Me. Don't say these things. Don't speak these things out loud.* But I say, 'I'm fine . . . I'm just fine, please.'

And David touches my shoulder with his nimble, anaesthetist fingers, and says quietly, 'You are not fucking fine, Jennifer. Stop lying to yourself.'

I am crying then. 'What are you saying? How can you say these things?' And he pulls me in close and holds me, and my relief is vast, it is primordial.

When I pull away I feel unsteady, not knowing exactly what I'm looking at, what he sees, what has happened. I tell him he should go, that we'll talk after a rest, after some time. So he does go, telling Sam he's been called in. And Sam and I eat our cake in silence, watching the end of the film, and then we fall into our empty beds.

At 5 am I drive Sam to the airport. The ocean and sky are navy blue glass holding back stars and a lingering moon. We drive past ghost-lit factories, past sprawling cages of steel, gardens of silent smoke and light. Sam is a silhouette next to me. She tells me how she once went to a small theatre alone, and standing by the ticket booth she met an Italian man who was gorgeous, educated, divorced and forty-two. He asked her out, but she didn't go.

'A chance meeting, how romantic. What a pity you said no,' I say, my eyes on the road and the long line of reflectors that stretch out in front of us. I am thinking that my house will be empty when I get back from the airport. 'When did that happen?'

'Oh,' she says, 'last week.'

I spin my head and face her briefly. 'Are you *crazy?*' I say, then straighten my steering. 'Why didn't you say *yes?*'

'I'm not sure. I felt guilty that I was going to spend the weekend with the Norwegian.'

'*What?* How could you chuck away such an opportunity?'

'I still have his number . . . I just . . . forgot that I had it.'

I glance at her again. She is smiling in the darkness. 'He was really good-looking.' Sam laughs. Her hands, for the first time, dance in the air. 'I know! We can have a Cinderella theme for the wedding . . . I'll wear glass slippers.'

I think about brides in glass slippers – it is such an apt metaphor, and yet none of the little girls know it. *Tiptoe away from the ball,* we should tell them. *Mind your step as you make your wary way down that aisle.*

I say, 'You'll wear Manolos, not glass. And I'll make sure you turn up.'

We drive through all the dark industry: as cold and leering as it is dependable. I am thinking about Matthew, about David, about Burma. I see my hands on the steering wheel, my knuckles white and tense. I wonder if the sun in Burma would turn my skin golden, give my fingers their old curve. Could you have babies in Burma? Cup their head in your golden palm, swaddle them to your chest? The thought tears into me like a Charismatic revelation, and I could stop the car, crawl out and weep with my eyes in the dirt. Disaster is complacency plus time, cowardice plus time, and I have been such a coward. I drive on, and a pale light perfuses the sky.

'I'm really glad I came,' says Sam, turning to me, smiling.

It had seemed so early in the day when we left the house – and for such a long time – early enough to live forever. And now I am thinking about my beautiful friend David, and all that he has offered, and I couldn't answer Sam even if I wanted to, so swollen am I with heat and with life from his radiant Burmese sun.

April is the Cruellest Month

There were lumps growing under my T-shirt, new hairs in my undies, Year Seven was half over and this chick turns up with a five-page vocational questionnaire. The reason we had to do it, announced Mr Josh, our homegroup teacher, was to 'guide us in our high-school trajectory'. Apparently this was the trajectory that would lead us to our lives, and as such it warranted scientific calibration in the form of this questionnaire. Mr Josh pointed round the room with his missile finger and made his serious, rat eyes. 'Be brutally, brutally honest here, kids, or you might take off on the wrong life.'

I picked up my pen; curious, excited. I was dying to know what I'd be. But the questions didn't seem vocational: *Do you like to look in the mirror? Do you find yellow serene?* I only had the options of 'sometimes', 'always', or 'never', and pretty soon a pattern emerged: my answer for every single question was 'sometimes'. Perhaps there was some kind of mistake? With me or with the questionnaire, who knew? But Mr Josh had insisted on honesty and honestly, *sometimes* I liked to look in the mirror, and *sometimes* I avoided it like a strange smell from an oily boy. And yellow, as if there was only one yellow. Sunlight: serene. Piss: not serene. Bananas: depended on the context.

The wind bullied the windows and I started to sweat my new sweat, that dampness which usually had me running to the loos to scrub under my arms with wet toilet paper. But there was no time for personal hygiene, my entire future was at stake here. I stared at the questions until my eyes spasmed in panic: 'sometimes' was always the answer. Then time was up and the chick packed the forms into a box and took them away for computer analysis. Afterwards, I casually questioned a few girls in my class; unlike me, they had not always picked 'sometimes'.

Mr Josh was a fat ex-Catholic with messy, red hair. First thing each morning, for the entire year, he'd read a line or two from *The Waste Land*, and try to make the class discuss it. The discussions went like this: blank stares, surreptitious spitballs, snorts, and Kylie. Kylie's favourites: 'Look around you, Josh, what's poetry got to do with anything about anything anymore?' or 'If he's so great, why can't he just say it straight: the world sucks and then you die.'

I found the poem sometimes thrilling, sometimes terrifying, sometimes tedious and most of the time opaque. Flesh wrinkled and sagged and then rotted. There were bones, bones, and more bones: dry, buried, picked and lost. Breasts were jugs or duds, and they drooped from the chests of old men. I sat there as Mr Josh read and the words crept around my skin, shaking parts of my body, waking them, shaming them, reminding me they were there or were coming there soon, or else would soon be gone. I learned a bit of trivia, too: Italian roosters crowed Co-co-rico, rather than the idiotic Cock-a-doodle-do. And outside it may have been winter, but my body had definitely hit April.

Two weeks later we skipped Eliot and Mr Josh handed out the envelopes with our results from the questionnaire. I held my breath and cracked mine open like a fortune cookie.

1. *Teacher*
2. *Author*
3. *The Clergy*

There was no commentary. I could take it or leave it. The list, Mr Josh explained, was a scientifically sound guide to a suitable career path.

How many nun jokes are there? The answer is millions, and the boys in my class knew them all. That day I rejected science and its poxy vocational suggestions. A teacher? A writer? The *clergy*?

Nuns, I'd read somewhere, weren't allowed to swim or compete. So that day, I decided to be a champion swimmer. Step one was getting the bus to Myer after school and buying my first swimsuit. I texted Mum, told her I'd be late, and chose red bathers in case I got my period unexpectedly. I'd had it twice so far: blood out of nowhere, appearing on the toilet paper like a yelp in the dark, the dull ache in my pelvis coming only later in the afternoon. The lot of it explaining my tears the day before, ostensibly shed over the mobile phone ads on TV, or a dead flower, or some carrot peelings lying limp on the sink. What was wrong with me? Oh, *that* again. I imagined the walk from poolside to change rooms would be less humiliating with a little colour-camouflage. I planned to start training that weekend.

Overall, I didn't mind school and I thought I'd hang around until I was officially selected for the Australian Olympic team. Most of the time I liked English best and I'd just finished an essay on the differences between human beings and animals. We'd been reading

Animal Farm. I'd overheard the principal telling Mr Carpenter not to let the discussions get too political, and so maybe that's why our essay was on animals versus humans.

'Physically, we share much with animals: we are born, enter puberty, menstruate, mate, and die,' I wrote. 'The major difference between an animal and a human is the fact that animals can't speak, they can't make things happen, they can't plan, or say no. Unlike the human, an animal can't think about its life as having a beginning, middle and end.'

When Mr Carpenter read my essay he rubbed his beard and said, 'Lisa, your sentences are far too long.'

This was not the sort of feedback I'd expected, but I recovered. 'Too long? Dickens wrote sentences that took up an *entire page.*' I spread my arms out wide.

Mr Carpenter smiled and looked down at me. He said, 'Yes, Lisa, that may be quite true, but *you* are not Dickens.'

No, I wanted to say, you're quite right. Dickens didn't get bloody underpants at random intervals, for a start.

I took the bus to the Footscray Pool on Saturday morning. I stood in the spectator stand in a cloud of hot chlorine and looked down on a cesspool of lycra. There was only one lane for lap swimmers. In that lane were three old women with elephant-skin necks holding perms above yellow kickboards, and one ancient skeleton doing a breaststroke that blocked traffic both ways. Two puffed-up, dunce-eyed pregnant women in life jackets – their alarming white bellies and boobs so big I could see them through the murk – jogged on the spot in the deep end. It was no place for a future champion swimmer, but I had no choice. I imagined the headlines: World Champion Was Once Forced To Train in Squalor. I checked my undies were all clear, pulled on my bathers, grabbed a kickboard and slipped into the warm water.

I hadn't swum since Year Four, since just before I missed the National Junior Brownies' swimming carnival. I'd been signed up for six events and I boasted to Mum and Dad about how I'd be in the most races at Brownies, then completely forgot about it. That is, until one Saturday afternoon, Dad stopped his car at a red light and I looked over and saw Narelle Mouldy eating a Polly Waffle in the back seat of her mum's station wagon, with her hair all wet. We were going in the same direction as the Mouldys, but they'd been at the Brownies' swimming carnival – where Tracey Briscoe had had to be me, as well as herself – and we'd been at Nan's, for roast lunch. Just before the realisation of what I'd forgotten drowned my brain in guilt and shame, I felt this ferocious regret; it pushed my organs around, searching for places to lodge. It pummelled me and it whispered, *You could have been a champion.*

I pushed off and kickboarded up rat's alley. There were obstacles: other lap swimmers; the old man with rattling bones; the pregnant women, sated as pigs and psychotically oblivious to anything but their bellies. I had to hover in the deep end for a full minute clearing my throat before they got the hint and heaved the bellies to one side. I made a strategic decision: I turned around, closed my eyes and charged. I felt the surface slap at my feet, the water shower my head, the muscles in my thighs burn. In moments my board hit the lane's other end. I gulped for air. The preggers women moved to the recreation lanes, old bones disappeared and the grannies drifted to the fringe.

At home, over dinner, I announced my new career.

Mum pushed a blob of mashed potato onto her fork. 'Well, dear, you know you can always come and work at the post office with me.'

Dad told me to pass him the salt.

About a week after the trajectory questionnaire, Mr Josh asked me to come to his office – a windowless, book-lined nook at the back of the classroom.

He slumped into his chair and said, 'Lisa, what are you planning to do with your life?'

I looked at my shoes. All I could think of were Eliot's repeated words: HURRY UP PLEASE IT'S TIME. HURRY UP PLEASE IT'S TIME. Time for a decision, time to leave the pub, time from one end of the pool to the other.

'You need to think seriously about your future and plan your subject selection accordingly. Have you considered teaching, for example?'

I looked at him. 'The computer suggested that.'

He nodded. 'With a bit of determination you could do quite well. But you need to decide if you'll stream into Science or Art, and get serious about your studies.'

I looked up at the spines of the books on his shelf and said, 'TS Eliot worked as a bank clerk.'

Mr Josh looked grave. He said, 'Yes, Lisa, but *you* are not TS Eliot.'

I upped my training schedule. I took the bus to the swimming pool each afternoon, hiding my zits under my fringe, panicking that I'd get my period and have to turn around and come home. You couldn't swim with a pad the size of a surfboard stuffed in your Speedos. I sat behind yellow-haired women with chins like hairy sausage rolls; behind stinking, splay-legged men. They all discussed how it was almost summertime, their pet cats' stupid habits and the electricity bills come winter again. 'Gas,' someone would invariably suggest, 'gas is much cheaper.'

I stared out of grimy bus windows, at endless streams of squat house-fronts, huddled together under violet skies. To zoom past them was like fanning the pages of a book with tiny pictures drawn in the corner of every page; when each image differed only ever so slightly from the one prior, the effect was of something moving in slow motion. The sun could rise and set, dull roots could sprout and grow, a gate might even creak open.

I wrote a story about a girl who wins ten gold medals at the Sydney Olympics. At the presentation ceremony she looks out at the crowd and sees the faces as circles, and the eyes and mouths on the faces as circles within the circles. She stands watching this sea of circles and realises she is made of circles, too, and that the crowd probably sees her as circles within a circle. She looks down at her chest full of medals. She looks up at the Olympic symbol. She starts to tremble. She whispers: *Everything is a circle.*

Mr Carpenter said he thought parts of the story were quite good. 'But I think the end is obscure. Shouldn't she just accept flowers and win major advertising deals?'

Apparently that was funny.

I stared at him.

He wiped his eyes.

I crossed my arms and drummed my fingers against my elbow. 'Mr Carpenter, I thought you'd read *Finnegans Wake*?' I'd looked it up on Wiki: an obscure book, sort of in English.

He pulled at his collar. 'Well . . . yeess . . .'

'So, regarding "obscurity",' I said, 'what about Joyce?'

His recovery was instantaneous. 'Lisa, Lisa, Lisa.' He shook his head. '*You're* not —'

'I *know*!' I cut across him and slammed my folder shut.

At school my friends discussed which department of Myer they'd work in. They discussed shaving their legs, pimple creams, bra sizes and tampons. My mum had forbidden me from using tampons until I was fifteen, for reasons unspecified, and she wouldn't let me use Impulse spray deodorant, bras or shavers. No one was interested in discussing my latest lap time, brands of goggles or the appalling state of the Footscray Pool. I took to wearing baggy jumpers which covered my bum, in case I leaked, and I read novels at lunchtime, counting down the hours till I could hit the pool. No matter how crappy, misshapen and clumsy I felt, when I put on my swim cap and bathers and walked poolside, I was queen. I could swim, and in the water, that was all that counted.

And there were moments: the late sun directly touching lane six so that the bubbles streaming from my fingertips rolled into pearls, and my arm turned molten gold. Or some hairy man trying to race me and we touch the end together, but I tumble turn and keep on going and he hangs over the edge, hacking for air like an old dog. Some days I'd forget where I ended and the water began; I'd think I could breathe it right in. A few times I had the entire pool to myself, and the only sound in the room was the sound that I made.

I wrote a story about a girl who has an eye disease that gives her patchy vision. She stands in her room and the window is a blur of light, the carpet an indeterminate smear of green, a silver flash on the wall is her mirror. From the corner of her eye she sees the knotted flowers in the tapestry of her armchair: each stitch, the bunched fibres of every thread. On her fuzzy brown desk, the title of a book looms and twists on its pale spine. The black letters mutate and swell as if seen through a gyrating magnifying glass. The title is the entire alphabet, A to Z.

I put the story in the bottom drawer of my desk, kicked the drawer closed and sneered 'Lisa, Lisa, Lisa' in Mr Carpenter's voice.

My training progressed. I could swim a kilometre of free-
style. I had girl biceps. I watched the Sydney Olympics
on TV and realised that it took me exactly three times
longer than the champions to swim a lap. I started to
panic, but then decided to be mathematical about the
whole thing.

I assembled my textbooks and a blank sheet of paper.
I worked out that based on my rate of improvement thus
far – utilising a fractionated linear equation, a differential
formula that allowed for exponential slowing of development with time, and adjusting for normal age-related
physical degeneration – I had reached my peak level of
performance exactly one month ago.

I chewed the end of my pencil, double- and triple-
checked the figures. They were rock solid.

The trouble with mathematics was it never helped you
formulate Plan B. I searched elsewhere for direction. I read
The Prime of Life, Mrs Dalloway and *Jane Eyre*. I read *Oliver
Twist* and *Krapp's Last Tape*. Accidentally, I read *The Diary
of Anaïs Nin*. None was particularly vocational. I searched
glossy magazines by the checkout: skeletal women with
tight faces, their bones slunk in silk. Big brunettes with
bare teeth and breasts, laughter sliding down their long
milky throats. They were all so smooth and clean, not
a pimple or pad amongst them, and I bet they smelled
like bright department stores. There were directors and
musicians, movie stars and singers. How did they get that
polish? What did they study to become them?

I kept swimming. I knew my professional career was over, but I had nothing else. On the bus I listened to the ladies discuss the price of petrol, the price of chops, the price of beige support pantyhose. And gas, invariably all conversations came down to the cheap price of gas. So that I didn't go out of my mind, I read.

Thankfully, I hadn't had my period for two months, but when I caught myself crying over a Britney Spears headline, I took decisive action. Hot and sweaty with shame and excitement, I snuck into the bathroom with a jar of Vaseline, four of Mum's tampons and the instruction booklet from the pack. I put a mirror on the floor, stood with my feet on either side and poked around. It wasn't real pretty down there – sparsely forested, pink and red madness, like there'd been half a bushfire. It took me three attempts: Vaseline all over the place, a dry white lump forced most of the way inside. But I was not going to let some gross inconvenience bully me out of my pool.

I wrote an Art essay, sitting at my desk, annoying a bleeding zit on my chin. I read and thought and wrote, and tried to rise above my errant body. 'While it's true that beauty is in the eye of the beholder, that can't be the final word unless we expand "the beholder" to include a city, a country, an era. If the idea of beauty was fixed there would be no need for fashion. But if we only had fashion we'd only need shops: there would be no need for galleries and libraries.'

I showed the rough draft to my Art teacher, Mr Brett. He had long black hair and wore crazy old paisley ties. He started chuckling as he read. I folded my arms tight across my big jumper, steeled for *Lisa, Lisa, Lisa, but you are not beautiful*. He looked up from my pages and said, 'Lisa, this is great.' And he went to his office and came back with a paperback by a man named Harold Bloom.

A big brown muscle man started swimming each day at the same time as me. He wore long black flippers and held heavy rubber disks in his hands. He always got in my lane and spent the entire time overtaking me. I didn't know if he was a psychopath or a paedophile. I didn't even know if I was too old now for paedophiles. I'd woken one morning last week and found a crop of pubes growing on the wrong side of my undies. I'd stolen one of Dad's plastic green razors. The whole thing was shameful: was it normal to get hair there? Could everyone see the stubble? Should I do my legs, too? Would it make the hair grow back thicker? Was I turning into a yeti? I wondered all this as I swam back and forth, dodging the bully and his gear. One time he swooped past and I didn't move aside fast enough; the edge of his flipper caught me in the mouth and made a deep gash in my lip. I stood up, stunned, and bled into my cupped, wet hands.

From then on I would quietly change lanes whenever he got in. That is, after I accidentally kicked him hard in his Speedos the very next time he overtook me. I felt that soft squash against hard bone beneath my toes – and the thrill of revenge – for weeks afterwards.

At night I'd stare at the pale wall in front of my desk, lick at the slowly healing cut on my lip, and try not to think about the future. I couldn't imagine a time when I'd know enough to teach or write anything. And there was no department of Myer I felt I could face day after day. Maybe the clergy was the answer, after all.

One afternoon, a few weeks before summer holiday, Mr Brett took me to the university library to find books about the Surrealists. I'd asked a few questions and he thought I could do with higher quality information than the school library offered. It was the first time I'd been to the university. We walked over cobblestones and the last of the spring petals and Mr Brett pointed out the old buildings he'd once studied in. We walked through a grass quadrangle and under the branches of a cherry plum still in full bloom, pale green leaves competing with the flowers. Everywhere I looked there were students in sunlight – writing, debating, drinking coffee, lying asleep with books shielding their eyes from the sun. In the Art Department's library, Mr Brett sat me at a study carrel and brought me book after book.

On our way out he said, 'Oh hey, I almost forgot, I wanted to show you the sports centre.'

We walked into a cavernous, geometric glass building. The receptionist said we could take a look around. The pool was unbelievable: the water looked blue and cool, without a whiff of chlorine, and there were *twelve* lanes just for laps. Mr Brett said, 'You can become a member here if you want. It's not very expensive.'

The next day, after intense parental negotiations about the health advantages of a non-chlorinated, state-of-the-art, saltwater pool, and with the membership fee in an envelope deep in my pocket, I took the bus way past Footscray and got off near the university.

I found the glass building, filled in the forms, paid my money and walked straight to the change rooms without anyone stopping me. All the girls were older and taller than me. Like a pride of Amazons, they blithely slipped in and out of their bathers, exposing neat triangles of thick hair, pert or heavy breasts, shaved and not-shaved armpits, all of which I tried not to study. They blow-dried their hair and rubbed on rosy lip gloss. No one gave me a second look, but I couldn't do it like them, not yet. I changed in a toilet, wrapped myself in my towel and crept poolside.

I slunk out of my towel, chose a lane and quickly dived in. My limbs sliced through the still water. I picked up speed, carved back and forth, and after a while I no longer saw water, or the lines marking my lane. Instead, in front of my eyes someone flicked the pages of a thick, old book. There was a small girl drawn at the top corner of each page, and as the pages were fanned, she soared through a line of hoops. Like a giant, she leapt and hurdled. My heart hammered and the pages cascaded. The faster I swam, the faster they tumbled, and I watched that little figure dive through hoop after hoop, her body stretched, her hair flying, pearls streaming from her fingertips.

I dressed and walked back through the university grounds. I stood outside the open gates with my hair all wet and my bag full of sopping swimgear. Students strolled in, students strolled out. Crowds of them: chatting, dreaming, reading as they walked. I stood my ground, tucked my wet hair behind my ears and picked up snatches of conversation. And believe me, no one was talking about gas.

Some Kind of Fruit

The day before I left Rome I saw three robbers guillotined . . . The first turned me quite hot and thirsty, and made me shake so that I could hardly hold the opera-glass (I was close, but was determined to see, as one should see everything, once, with attention); the second and third (which shows how dreadfully soon things grow indifferent), I am ashamed to say, had no effect on me as a horror, though I would have saved them if I could.

– Lord Byron, 1817

It was medical school before the era of snuff-medicine TV. Before surgery and sawn-off shotgun wounds hit prime time. I'd come into contact with live flesh, but the sick and infirm, the dead, I had only seen depicted by Old Masters. I wanted to be a psychiatrist, and I heard there'd been a revolution, a new trend for Medicine-and-the-Arts, and that you no longer needed Science or Maths to get in. They wanted students who'd lived a little, who thought a little, who could speak in full sentences human to human. For some reason they thought a Humanities degree was a guarantee of those things. And so, my degree in Art History – the one everyone told me was pretty, but useless – ushered me right in.

James and I made friends on day one of med school, recognising each other instantly: two old hags who wanted to be shrinks, searching for unscorched coffee.

'Heather,' I smiled.

'James,' he smiled.

And we were inseparable.

For a year, both of our boyfriends lived interstate; we shared a ride to the airport every second weekend. He flew to Queensland. I flew to Melbourne. During the week we cooked dinner and studied at his apartment. He had an ocean view; my bedsit didn't have a working stove. He always had cake: orange and spice, raspberry and coconut, chocolate, hummingbird. He was an English Lit graduate with a stomach as delicate as my own.

Despite the revolution, there were mainly three types of med student. Anorexic gym bunnies who came from the School of Dietetics and Physiotherapy. Computer geeks with bad skin. And the majority: bland, clean-cut Christians; that sea of neat brown hair. James and I sat at the back, to the left, near the exit, so we could move out as fast as possible.

In first year we struggled with anatomy. The wet lab reeked of recirculated formaldehyde. Dissected body parts were stored in vats with texta signs: *Arms, Legs, Torsos, Heads with Neck*. The flesh hung from the bones in wet grey strings, the yellow tendons intact. We stood back, shoulder to shoulder, while students pretty as soap opera stars huddled around the stainless steel tables in lurid gloves. One of them pulled a tendon and made a finger curl. He looked at us sideways and said we'd learn nothing from way over there. I told him I was learning plenty. Under his breath James said, 'Jesus Christ, Heather, he must be what, twelve?'

I bought Rohen and Yokochi's *Human Atlas*, the heaviest book on the planet. Its pages felt like cool water. They were printed on both sides with full colour, high definition photographs of newly dead bodies in perfect slices, red muscles deflected with steel forks.

'Who needs tendons?' I said to James as we peered into its depths. 'Yeah,' he said twisting his neck to get a different angle, 'who needs tendons?' And the old man with the peeled face on page 165 taught us the muscles of mastication.

I looked at the *Atlas* each night before bed. A drama of epic proportions. I got to know the bodies: their age, their sex, their race. The dissections were exquisite: so tender, the deepest layer of the neck with the spinal cord and medulla exposed. So vulnerable, the chest when split, leaving heart and lungs bare. The Japanese man on page 320, his eyes closed, thick thighs open. Impressive. I would gaze down at my skin and understand what it held at bay: a story with the most intricate of plots.

James recalled a Cultural Studies lecturer claiming that the inside of a body was just a big mess. She'd said it was medicine which constructed the organs; that really, there was no such thing – in and of itself – as 'a spleen'. We scanned page 205 for her: *Posterior abdominal wall with duodenum, pancreas and spleen.* We signed it 'Anonymous Universal', and sent it by express mail. I found the whole thing amusing, but it made James really mad. 'Cultural relativism,' he kept spitting. 'Social constructivism,' he'd curse. 'The body exists! The body exists!' He'd thump his chest like a madman and yell it at me, as if I didn't know.

We went to the national med students' conference to dance. Each night we took a pill some boy from Sydney Uni had cooked. He winked when we asked him what they were, and told us to remember his name (some kind of fruit). James and I argued about whether the crumbly pills were amphetamine or E. We took each other's tachycardic pulse, we sweated, we laughed. James would scream, 'Science is truth!' from the dance floor, while we boogied fury on muscles we knew the *Atlas*'s names for. We slept in the same bed from six till ten, then rose, cleared our throats and called our boyfriends: *Yes . . . It's good . . . You know. Just conference stuff.*

Towards the end of first year, James's boyfriend moved in with him and my boyfriend decided we had drifted apart. He'd had a short story published in a journal and was hanging around people who wore interesting glasses. He said he didn't want to move, and besides, he felt he couldn't go out with someone who'd joined an Ideological State Apparatus. 'But I'm going to be a shrink!' I told him. He said those were the worst offenders.

I felt gutted. The image of my future consulting room – with its leather couch, still air and abstract expressionist oil paintings – cracked up. But James rolled his eyes when I told him and made me mail the prick a copy of the spleen.

They assessed us relentlessly. Name. Define. Diagnose. Extrapolate and deduce. Examine, report, explain, memorise, tick-the-right-fucking-box. 'I'm no scientist,' I'd threaten James. 'I've always hated Science,' I'd argue. He'd just nod and feed me bigger slabs of cake.

We'd study hard then take a break. He'd go swimming, and I'd wander the National Gallery, visiting old friends on the walls, getting myself lost and found. I'd stand in front of Frankenthaler and squeeze and wring my hands. *I could have lived here, searching for words,* I implored her dilute paint on un-primed canvas. Wring. Squeeze. Instead, I'd joined an Ideological Apparatus. James swam. I wrung my hands for answers. James's deltoids hypertrophied. Security ushered me out at 6 pm each night.

There were little distractions. The intern named Fred with the skinny ties and stove-pipe pants who started off teaching me my heart sounds and ended up lifting my blouse right up over my head. The Cardiologist –

unnamed – who liked to torque me to the reserve in his ancient, silver Porsche. He'd lay a crisp white napkin over his Armanis and I'd climb on board. He'd knead me and knead me, 'You're so sexy, you're so sexy.' But what about lovable? I wanted to ask.

I spent what money I had on make-up, shoe paint and vintage belts. I became obsessed with lip gloss and would test them out on James. 'Whuddayathink?' I'd ask and pout, and he'd take his time to answer. I bought one called 'Strawberry Fields' and told him to have a smell. He closed his eyes and leaned in close, almost touching his nose to my lips. 'They smell like childhood . . . Your lips smell exactly like childhood.' And his eyes, when he raised them, were all out of focus.

Our Biochemistry lecturer was a psychopath. We tried to get interested, but lipids and amino acids and the Krebs cycle and DNA – although potentially thrilling, the very stuff of life – became monotonous chaff when ground through his mouth. If you asked him a question it only got worse, and the answers were certainly not English. I'd look at James and ask, 'Why?' He'd look at me and ask, 'Why?' We came up with a stock answer: *so-we-can-be-psychiatrists-comma-so-we-can-spend-our-lives-exploring-the-mind.*

By third year it had got to the point where I was no longer sure what was me and what was not. James, too, seemed smudged around the edges, like a line drawing smeared with wet fingers. It was almost mid-year exams.

We took to dancing. Cheap red instead of dinner, studying over pots of espresso. In between sessions I would be gripped by terrifying questions. *Does tricuspid incompetence lead to a murmur in systole or diastole? At what dose will hydralazine reach tachyphylaxis?* I'd ring James. His boyfriend, if he answered, would call out, 'James, it's your girlfriend,' and drop the phone on the floorboards.

But James was ringing me, too, breathing into the receiver, saying things like, '*Science*, Heather — Truth or Knowledge?' Or, 'Heather, I studied *Culture* . . . And now I study *Biology* . . .' I'd hang on the line waiting for his conclusion, but one was never forthcoming.

Occasionally, he'd ask me what I was wearing and I'd tell him in the third person, spinning pictures into words. 'Heather is wearing her black, skinny jeans, cut strategically low at the back . . .'

Once, he asked me if tonality was biological.

'Tonality?' I said.

'Yes,' he replied.

'Biological?' I said.

'Yes,' he replied.

I said I didn't know. Was making a flat canvas look 3-D biological? Was social-realist writing biological? He told me not to argue.

'I'm not arguing!' I said.

We'd drink and then we'd dance, banging hips, bone against bone. No one came near us. We were a universe; something framed and perfect. Him and Me.

On drinking nights we'd meet at my place and James would wait for me to get ready. I'd stand splay-legged in my bra and skirt flinging clothes from my washing basket. 'It's in here somewhere. I know it's in here some-where.' One time James said he would wait downstairs. I stopped mid-fling and straightened up with my palm on my back. 'What's up?' I asked him.

He ran out the door with his eyes on the carpet and his cheeks all red. I stared at the door, shuffling explanations. I looked down at my bra (a lacy black number the Cardiologist had sent me from Paris). I laughed and shook my head. 'I don't look that bad!' I beseeched the empty room, my arms stretched out wide.

Fag Hag is such an unappealing term, but my distrac-tions were now few and generally married. I did like the older man. But I also liked the younger man. The equi-aged man. And men in general. 'I'm just not girlfriend material,' I complained to James. Then my mouth ran riot about how girls with any cynicism scared men off; about brains and personal direction being taboo; about my refusal to play idiotic games. James started to laugh, his red lips pursed. 'Is it perhaps because you're taken?' he asked. Then he laughed some more.

And we passed. Like diluted paint on un-primed canvas, the stuff had seeped in and spread; amalgamated, cohered with barely any willing on our part. But I was in the grip of a crisis I could no longer ignore. So, in second semester, I secretly overloaded my course and enrolled in the Philoso-phy of Science and Art. The lecturer was a quiet man who looked a lot like a jockey. Popper. Kuhn. Greenberg. Fry. What was Science? What was Art? What was I doing in med school at all? I wrote my essay on Rohen and Yokochi, on their aesthetic masterpiece of patience and technique. I split the essay in two. In part one I argued the book was Science (Rohen and Yokochi had possessed a scary knowledge of where to cut; they found arteries no one knew existed). In part two I argued it was Art (purity, light, form). I let the two rest side by side; who ever said something had to be only one thing or the other? James thought I was a genius. The jockey wasn't convinced.

I skipped the gallery and started swimming with James. I'd swim for fifteen minutes then sit in the stands watching him slice through the blue. I loved to watch him; that fierce stroke and muscular back, his regular gasps for air. I realised I'd rather look at him than at 'Blue Poles', than 'The Death of Marat', than Frankenthaler, Kokoschka or Klee. I realised I loved to watch him; that he'd become my kind of aesthetic. Hopeless grief: my old familiar. If I loved a gay man what did that make me? A gay male? Confusion was just the beginning. This was worse than adolescence.

When his boyfriend was at work we'd hang out in the kitchen and James would bake us cakes. A shelf of mixed books hung above his kitchen bench: *The Thief's Journal*, Stephanie Alexander and *The Norton Anthology of Poetry*. I'd browse and he'd cook and sometimes I'd read to him, little snippets. One week it was chocolate and hazelnut and I tipped out a book on Queer Theory.

'What exactly is Queer Theory?' I asked, turning the glossy book over, looking for a summary.

'Not what it used to be,' he said and buried himself further in his recipe. 'Can you pass me those hazelnuts? And line this pan with paper.'

'Yes, sir, right away.' I went to pass him the nuts, but snatched them back at the last moment. 'I explained neo-classicism for you!'

'Heather, it's a rancid can of worms, okay? An old, rancid, can of worms.' And he looked so dark, like the blackest corner of an oil painting, one that might hide something or might not, and it was strange to see him pouring sugar with that look on his face.

In final year we did a semester of Obstetrics and Gynaecology. We had to assist in three operations and watch three deliveries. I stood next to a young father and watched his face fill with horror as their daughter tore her way through his young wife's legs. I watched a seventy-year-old lady have a total pelvic evisceration and I subsequently missed my period. I remembered my pet guinea pig, with the ginger and white fur. It had what I thought was a period – left these horror-inducing little strings of blood and mucus all around its hutch – and then, the next morning, I'd found her stiff on her back, hunkered up next to the water dripper. And all I'd felt was relief. I was rid of her, she was gone; the bleeding thing was gone.

I told James about my missed period. He asked if I was pregnant. I raised an eyebrow. 'Yeah,' I said. 'With baby Jesus.'

It had been a long time between distractions.

'That's too bad,' he said.

My head veered backwards. 'Are you crazy?' He told me he desperately wanted a baby, a little tiny baby. I relaxed and I laughed.

'I'm serious,' he said. My laugh flipped to stutter.

'I'm serious,' he said, and his eyes followed suit.

'With who, what? Are you crazy?' I asked, my stomach now something deranged. 'I . . . I've seen these women lose their *gonads* for Christ's sake, James! I've seen them *blown to bits.*'

'Blown to bits,' he quietly repeated, some old sadness in his eyes.

We studied for our final long-case. The wards were packed with students practising on all the available patients, so James and I went to my place and took turns on each other.

'So, James, you are obviously in a critical condition,' I giggled. 'Please remove your shirt and your jeans. Now lie back and breathe.'

I put my hand on his beautiful shoulder and pressed my stethoscope to his heart; it beat faster and faster and I could barely hear it over my own. I cleared my throat, looked to his face and proclaimed his heart normal.

'Normal,' he repeated, and brushed his fingers across my lip gloss. I felt his breath on my face. He said, 'You make me feel like a child in a playground.' And then he kissed me, lightly, on the lips. Utter bewilderment didn't come close.

'James . . .' I said.

'Well . . .' he answered.

And – like the rest – he belted his jeans, and went home. We resolved it all quickly, by laughing and blaming the exams – those harbingers of madness and confusion. But it seemed to me that it was not so clear-cut, although the sums – James plus Heather, Heather plus James – all resisted their solutions. I liked men, James liked men: between us then there was only one thing missing.

At the end of semester we had a lecture on transsexuality. They figured we were ready, and what the hell, the content wasn't examinable. The Professor of Gynaecology was an old-school fag who wore ties with insignia. He displayed a pre-op male-to-female like a rat in a cage.

'This is Rachel,' he said in his clipped Oxford accent, pointing to a thin blonde in a polyester skirt-suit.

One of the Christians in the class went berzerk and turned on the professor. 'You're treating a mental illness with surgery! You've forged a disease out of thin air! We are *born* male or female, it's *chromosomally* determined!'

The professor stretched his pale neck, ever so slightly. 'These people,' he replied, 'are not easy to treat. These people have a high rate of suicide. These people attempt the surgery on themselves.'

The professor continued, discussing the intersexed, the sex hormones and their dysregulation. He said that the treatment of transsexuals was a work in progress, that we should think of the treatment as a working hypothesis in the face of immense suffering. He explained that the removal of the penis was a procedure covered by Medicare, but the subsequent construction of the vagina was not.

I leaned over to James. 'All of my boyfriends have turned out to be cunts.'

He looked at me and smiled, 'Well, Heth, that makes you a lesbian.' He raised his eyebrows up and down. 'And must have saved them a bit of cash.'

The professor projected slides of removal and reconstruction – penises made from abdominal flesh, and an attempt at a faux-vagina, a slowly expanding stent pushed into solid flesh.

That one made James flinch. 'Oh God, why do *that*? What's wrong with just taking it up the arse?' We sniggered behind our fists. There was a photo of a person with no genitalia at all, and it looked as disturbing as a mouth-free face.

'You know, I knew a lot of doctors were frustrated sculptors, but this, this is getting ridiculous!' I whispered.

'Ridiculous but also kind of amazing, don't you think?'

We studied the slides with alternating horror, amusement and reverence. When the professor finished, he asked us to show our appreciation to Rachel, so we all clapped. She blushed and bowed her head like a coquette, and the students burst into messy life, jumbled down the aisle, out the door. James and I lingered in our seats, watching Rachel and the prof.

James said, 'There's no reason we can't talk to her. Is there?'

I said, 'It would only be polite.'

James said, 'We wouldn't be doing anything wrong by just talking. Would we?'

I said, 'That wouldn't breech ethical boundaries at all.'

We made our way to the front and I found that I was shaking. She had tits and legs and I tried not to look at her skirt. What was she? Some kind of hybrid queen, in transition, momentarily having the best of both worlds. Cock plus tits plus lipstick. I was sick and shaken with envy and thrill.

'Hi,' said James. 'I'm James. This is Heather.'

Rachel cleared her throat, as if unsure of where to pitch her voice. 'Hello,' she said. Her long white fingers gripped and trembled; they were beautiful, both soft and masculine.

The professor picked up his shiny black Gladstone, nodded at Rachel and swept out of the room. For some reason I was surprised he left her all alone with us, although what did I expect? She was evidently of age.

'Thanks for coming,' said James.

'You're welcome,' said Rachel, girlish smile teasing her lips.

I studied her face. Subtle, clever make-up; not a trace of stubble. Her hair well-parted, glossy and long. This chick had studied her magazines. But there was something; she hadn't got it perfect – not yet, maybe not ever – something about the nose and the way it joined in and pulled at her face. That forceful nose screamed masculinity, made me wonder if she still had erections, despite all the oestrogen the professor pumped into her veins. I knew the answer was no, and I wondered, incredulous, didn't she miss it? Didn't she miss fucking like a man?

I asked her, 'Do you like coffee?'

'Sure,' she said. 'Sure I do.'

I looked at James.

'Join us?' he asked her.

She paused. 'Okay,' she said, voice up and down.

But for a few long seconds we stood there in our huddle – all breathing too fast, James and me both leaning in towards this fascinating creature – as if we'd all just had a good, long dance; or as if something big was about to happen. And I was dying to touch her: stroke her cheek, her torso, slip my hands between her bare legs, and see if all she had was as feather-down-shy as her manner. A hybrid queen, standing before us, and my fingertips ached to feel if it was true.

Tactics

In the eighties, it was Soft Cell and The Smiths. I was in love with Morrissey and hoped against all rumour that his croon was for me. Before then, it was the boy from our local grocery store, the one who helped shift the crates of sweating milk between the cool room and the fridges, cap pulled low over frantic blond hair, refusing to look at me whenever I walked past. Once or twice I dropped my school bag and stood right in his path, hands on what was fast becoming a waist. 'Look at me,' I screamed, or at least I really wanted to scream. He edged around me like I was just another crate.

The news about Morrissey, when confirmed in print, hit me and every other girl in 10C hard. That had Mr O'Shea chuckling to himself. A crush on a homo-sexual singer! Don't tell me you all couldn't see it? For a day, his chuckle skirted a sneer. After that, it was some-thing else. He'd stare out the window, blue eyes hovering above the car park, and let out these soft Irish noises we'd never heard him make before. He murmured like a poet, 'We are all so blind, so blind.'

Then Ben transferred to our school: a boy with lyrical understanding and the latest personal compact disc technology. It was the start of the-smaller-the-better, a new era. He was everything my family wasn't; a suburban exotic. We shared earplugs over ham and pickle sand-wiches; listened to the entire Cure library burned onto a plate of shining chrome. 'You're a real cool chick,' he said, and I thought we were progressing. He reintroduced me to The Smiths and spoke often of his lust for a Bang & Olufsen stereo with a flat remote and hidden speakers in every room. He never mentioned his lust for Rosa Mioli, the girl from 11B. She showed me the compilation tape – held it out in front of her two preposterous breasts – proving what she had, and that for her he was willing to use the old-fashioned.

I turned vegetarian to impress a girl called Jane. 'Forget guys,' she said, and loaned me her *Moosewood Cookbook*. I followed the cookbook prescription: sprouting my own mung beans for a superior protein; eating tofu as if I liked it. It took up stacks of my time. In free moments Jane studied for final exams and I hung out at Greville Street Records. The boys who worked there balanced records on their fingertips and stroked them like they were the back of a newborn's neck. I smiled like toothpaste ads and they took my cash, looking right through me, reluctant to let go of their babies. I bought my hardcore in vinyl: Bad Brains, and Rites of Spring, and Fugazi. I listened to them at home on Mum and Dad's plywood cabinet turntable. I listened all alone, wondering if there was a problem with my tactics. At Nan's house I'd watch dinnertime TV and eat roast lamb – she promised not to tell. It was nice there, anyhow, and it was almost time for uni.

Jane and I enrolled in our BAs in a university as far-flung from our suburb as possible. We moved together into a flat above a café. I read novels as if they were self-help. She read the radical feminists. I worked as a waitress; she cleaned five-star hotel rooms. By then it was the nineties and I was trying different tactics. So when a boy called Daniel showed up in my tutorial, sporting these big brown eyes and a vintage Bowie T-shirt, I acted like nothing had happened. I'd stare out the window with hovering eyes while the other girls sat next to him, looked up through their eyelashes and asked him questions about deconstruction. I moved around Daniel as if he were a crate. One day he cleared his throat and asked me if I had read *Nothing Exists But Still Somethings Exist*. I half turned my face towards him, eyebrows, nose and chin reaching angles Elizabethan. 'Yes,' I lied, 'I have.' And I turned back to my window.

Daniel asked me to The Lounge to see a band with fringe-type cultural capital. I wasn't sure what to wear and Jane was no help. She'd recently decided that clothes and boys and Lounges were patriarchal machinery. I chose archetypal things dyed black, and before I left, revised *Baudrillard for Beginners*.

Turns out Daniel and I agreed on the big three: *Neuromancer*, Joseph Cornell and *Hunky Dory* on vinyl. It was the era of the incommensurate.

Our meetings escalated. I went to his place – as small and neat as a converted ATM. I'd never before seen books meet top to toe. He arranged them by form rather than content. He had a titanium computer *and* a turntable. I couldn't beat his arguments and so we shared a couple of burgers, smoked imported cigarettes, aligned ourselves top to toe. And all night long we made a gentle kind of sense.

He came over to my place and precipitated thought experiments: Jane, willing him to death.

'De Beauvoir,' she'd say, slapping overcooked gnocchi into op shop bowls, 'rejected feminism outright when she crawled into the grave with Sartre.' We sat and listened to the slapping. She took the pan back to the kitchen and threw it at the sink.

'I'm not so hungry,' Daniel would murmur. For a boy, he had a sensitive stomach.

Things could have turned nasty, but Daniel won a scholarship for a year at UCLA. It was 'a fantastic opportunity', 'a once-in-a-lifetime experience', something he just *had* to do. It was the first time I'd heard him speak in clichés. I pictured blue skies and inordinate suns. I pictured Californian girls with breasts rounder than Rosa Mioli's. I didn't even know he'd applied.

So. What could I say? I turned my cheek and made it clear I had other things to do. I had books to read, film festivals to attend, papers to write, music to hunt out, clothes to dye. I had Jane. I had a boy called Simon in my Postmodern Narrative tutorial who was willing to come out and play. I drank macchiatos. Lamented past time. Worked hard to erase history. I was so busy I had to drop down to part-time study. Daniel's aerograms became mournful, then tragic, then frantic. He wrote in tiny clustered letters, between lines, in margins, around the space for the return address. I refused to get email, replied as slow as Tai Chi. *Life is fine,* I wrote to him. *Let's just be rational, philosophic. See what happens if it happens.* I was making the most of my assets.

Daniel came back at the end of autumn. Brown, crisp, beautiful. Towing a diploma in Cultural Studies and a marijuana habit bigger than Texas. At the time, these attributes were both considered valuable. His eyes went wet when he saw me and he said he wanted to share a house. I played it cool, weighed my options (though I'd decided straight away). Jane called me a fool. The Hungarian man who owned the café downstairs scratched his stubble, mopped his brow, and asked me what a 23-year-old baby was doing with a boyfriend, anyways.

I packed my records into crates and my clothes into garbage bags. A vegan named Chloe moved in with Jane and they both shaved off their hair. Daniel and I moved beachside. We each kept a separate bedroom-and-study. That way Daniel got to order things in his particular way, I could leave my frocks in bags and we'd choose where we'd sleep night by night. I was down to one subject a semester and losing momentum fast. Daniel was planning a thesis on a Frenchman named Deleuze. He planned all day, sitting on a Deco couch donated by my nan, rolling paper and herb between his white fingers, between splayed knees. He'd inhale hard, then stare at his imaginary thesis on the wall. I was right there with him. We were a duo of vague, ambitious staring, listening to Trance-diluted classics. It was the era of nostalgia.

Jane and Chloe invited us to dinner to announce the inevitable. Jane looked a bit thin, but they seemed happy together, domestic. After a few mugs of wine, Chloe admitted she liked the French Feminists. Daniel said they were philosophically sound. They discussed the dissolution of binary opposition; mysterious words like Kristeva and Cixous floated around us like *méthode champenoise*. Daniel faced Chloe, his finger curled around his chin like a question mark. Chloe met his eyes and gently licked a drop of wine from her wrist. I turned to a pillar of salt and stopped eating the lentils. Jane sat there like an evaporating binary.

Chloe moved out within the month. Daniel didn't come home most nights. Jane started a celery juice diet. She said it was for cleansing her liver. I told her she was the cleanest liver I knew, but she didn't get the joke and her shoulders stayed as slumped as my own. I said nothing to Daniel, pretended not to see. What else could I do?

Daniel's thesis supervisor suggested he commit a few thoughts to paper. Daniel came home and slumped on the Deco. He got up to make a bong out of an apple juice bottle and a length of plastic tubing. Smoke roared from his open lips. There was no music. Nights were days were nights. For two weeks, his focus stopped before it reached the wall. Then it sharpened. He looked at me sideways. When the phone rang, he would bolt to his feet, point between my eyes, tell me not to pick it up. Then he started talking about the unification of fire and water, about rhizomic thought capable of re-instigating the word; of parabolas reversing to make pathways for death. He didn't recognise me. I waved my fingers in front of his face and asked him if he could see. He said, 'I don't need to see to see.' When his eyes became pinwheels I called his parents, who called the community mental health team.

A psychiatrist put Daniel in the locked ward of a state psychiatric institution; he said that in his opinion the problem was drug-related and most likely temporary. Daniel slurred and dozed, slurred and dozed.

Our flat made me think of reversals carving pathways for death, so I stayed at Nan's house for a month, sleeping in the single bed of my childhood weekends, reading the magic realists, watching dinnertime TV on her new velour armchairs. She made us neat breakfasts and lunches and dinners. She urged me to study, and to wear a bit of lippy.

Daniel made no progress. His eyelids were mauve winter quilts. He looked at me, briefly – I was a crate, once again – before his parents closed in and carted him back to their house.

They gathered his books, his computer and turntable; left a month of rent and his bong in the middle of my carpet. Alongside a note telling me I was never to see Daniel again.

I went back to see Jane. What was left of her smiled at me from the open doorway. Her lips pulled her face behind her ears. She said, 'I'll just go for a little run before dinner.'

I sat in her lounge room staring at an imaginary friendship on the wall. Forty-five minutes later she came back and served herself a level cup of baked beans. 'They're the perfect food for me,' she said. 'Protein and carbohydrate and vegetable, all in one.' She shovelled fried rice and Peking duck from plastic containers onto my plate.

'Aren't you vegetarian?' I asked.

'Yes,' she said and smiled. 'But *you're* not.'

I put food in my mouth: teeth worked, throat refused. I forced the issue, tried not to cough.

'Jane . . .' I tried.

'So,' she cut through me, bright as an advertisement for soap, eating a neatly quartered bean, and making that ghoul grin again. 'How's things *with you?*'

I read Borges just lately. It was part of my latest tactic: sitting at Nan's by myself, as if I had a choice, as if I was fine, as if I could move any moment now. As if I had *sacks* of sane friends to spare. And I thought of how Borges went blind and recruited young people to read to him. They'd arrive at his house and he'd tell them what to read, then he'd sit there in his dark, sternly correcting their recitation. That was his lonely tactic.

So I sat there by myself, staring at nothing, book open flat on my lap. I thought of the golden labradors that lead the blind these days, getting them up and out of the house, licking their hands, loyally keeping them company. Jane hated the Guide Dogs Association with a scary sort of zeal. She raved about how the dogs weren't allowed to bark, nor howl, nor even whimper. She told me that to teach them that silence, the Association beat the dogs to bloody pulps. Sickos would join – she said – so they could beat up little pups.

'But . . .' I'd started to say, because I knew it made sense: how else could you get them to do what you wanted? You could offer them bones, withhold their water, wait and hope for a really long time. (I was quite familiar with such tactics.) Or, as an alternative, you could simply beat the living shit out of them. But I couldn't say that to Jane. So I said the other thing I thought: that surely the blind deserved them? Surely they deserved a man's best friend?

She'd bellowed over the top of me, 'Let the blind be blind and let the dogs act as they will.'

But, I had to disagree. Sometimes people need guidance! Sometimes people need a quiet and corrected best friend. So I closed my book and went online. I looked up the Guide Dogs Association. I was focused and smiling for the first time in years. I scrolled through their information until I found the right page, and – my fingertips tingling, my throat swelling with laughter, or with something – I signed up. As a hands-on volunteer.

Little White Slip

One litre of milk is enough for 40 cups of tea.
— *Presbyterian Women's Cookbook, 1955*

Black and White

She wears this nightie. A crisp, white cotton slip, plain as paper. It has thin white ribbons for shoulder straps. She wears it with trousers and ballet slippers during the day. (Telling herself it looks French.) And she wears it — without trousers or slippers, or that maternity bra — to bed. She has four, all identical, all filing through the wash one after the other. With the powder, brightener, softener, bleach. For the Whitest, Brightest Whites!

She used to be a little-black-dress kind of girl. Short black hemlines, short black espressos, short black nails, short sharp black bob. Elbows on the bar, one knee on the bar stool, nightlife ballet. A real G-string kind of girl. Little black sambuca shots screaming down her throat, while she waits for Frederik of Denmark, William of England, the French PM, to see her, to find her, to see her: shiny beanpole in the haystack. Tall amongst all that short.

Cheesecake

Her husband — an industrial chemist — flies to Melbourne for a weekend conference. Something to do with tempered precipitants and powdered solutions of some lethal substance or other. She hides her terror at being left alone with the baby overnight, and asks that he bring her back a slice of cheesecake from Acland Street.

You sure you'll be okay?

Just bring me the cake.

The really special Jewish one, baked from a 400-year-old recipe. She had it for breakfast once, aeons ago, not so long ago, tumbling out of a club into dawn, sambuca still cavorting with her tongue.

The night is long. She lies awake on their bed watching the baby twitch and dream. All the pillows are on the floor so it doesn't suffocate should she accidentally sleep; and to break its landing should it fall. When it wakes she pulls at a ribbon and guides her breast into its mouth. And it closes its eyes and it sucks and drinks, sucks and drinks, milk wetting its lips.

Her husband arrives home at midday, holding two white boxes wrapped in clear cellophane. He stands in the doorway. 'Ta-dah!' he says.

She blinks at the bright sun, and at her husband who blocks it inadequately, despite the two, vast boxes.

'What're those?'

'Your cakes!'

'Cakes?'

'The four hundred-year-old cheesecakes! From that Polish street! You know . . . Acland Street!'

'Tom.'

'Yes, honey?'

'I asked for a piece of cake. A *piece*? *One piece* of cake? You do realise I'm going to eat all of that.'

'Sure!'

'But Tom. Don't you see how fat I am?' She runs a hand down her slip, outlining her round belly.

'LouLou –' he balances the boxes in one hand, puts the free one around his wife '– you're not fat at all.'

'Sure, Tom.'

'You're not! You're beautiful! And you've just had a baby, for God's sake.' He turns around to grasp the handle of his suitcase.

'Sure sure sure sure sure. That's what they all say. And then you wake up and see the words *Barge Arse* listed on the divorce papers.'

He chuckles. His wife is so funny, such a great sense of humour. Ha ha ha ha ha.

She takes the butter-stained boxes – they're heavy, there must be six kilos of cheese in the fuckers – and stands aside to let him in.

'The baby's in the crib.'

Sambuca Dawn

'Well –' she brings the shot glass up close to her eye '– what exactly is sambuca, then, Doctor Smarty-Pants Chemist?'

So he wasn't heir-to-some-throne, oh no no he wasn't, but his eyes drew lines from the dark points of her nails and her lips and her sambuca and her hem. Dot to dot he traced her out, then coloured her in, buying her drink after drink.

'It's distilled Illicium verum.'

'Illicit whatum?'

'Illicium verum: star anise.'

'Oh,' she said, for some reason disappointed. 'I thought it was made out of liquorice.'

He apologised, as if it were his fault, which for all she knew it may well have been. Who the hell knew what industrial chemists were responsible for? And to compensate – for he was always compensating, bearing responsibility for some flaw in the world: ants in the rubbish, their combined carbon footprint, the inclement weather, a missed opportunity – he set about describing star anise, and the manner in which it was distilled, trying his best to make it sound beautiful, mysterious.

Meanwhile, she half-listened, drank her liquor with its floating beans of coffee, and weighed him up as best she could. Tall, clever, appreciative. Nice shoes, wide shoulders, appreciative. His eyes carved her out of the background. She drank drinks he paid for, and watched him carve her.

'It's eighty-four proof,' he was saying, 'so it's rather easily set alight.'

Clean shirt, white teeth, appreciative.

The Club

Laced around the café table, like round and fat beads of prayer: mother, pram, mother, pram, mother, pram. Everyone sweating into synthetic lace maternity bras. Sweat and milk swelling Hidden Absorbent Pads! Everyone's eyes behind oversized sunglasses. She's not sure who's being talked at. She's not sure who's listening. A particular way of pouting. She blames all this on Posh. The baby is asleep in its Bugaboo pram. Known in Louise's mind as The Ambulator. As in The Great Ambulator. As in The Really Fucking Expensive Ambulator. Lips peel open and relate brands of dummy, bowel habits and crying habits and sleep habits, and Louise stares into her orange juice, reluctant anthropologist, trying not to make nasty slips-of-the-tongue.

Screens 1

She sits at her desk when it sleeps again in its little fits and starts. *Yes, I am back at work . . . Part-time, of course. From home. Hmm? Yes, still Designing.* Capital D. *Still Web Page Designing.* In front of her shiny new Mac (white, seventeen inches). Another present from Tom. Another noose. Another dare. She's catalogued all their photos. Backed up the address book. Bought lollies from all over the planet (Duchy Mints, Hershey's Kisses, Iranian Toffee). She's written letters with too many exclamation marks that she'll never send to people she'll never see.

Today – making an effort, all her slips in the wash – she wears a black chiffon dress (huge, loose) with pearl-button detail and an emerald silk scarf. Shiny black ballet shoes. She loosens the belt again, crosses her legs, remembers varicose veins and uncrosses them. Hair up. Down. She adjusts her scarf and evaluates the weight of her breasts, estimates millilitres, translates into kilograms, or at least milligrams, takes that sum from her outrageous weight. She chews her pen, tightens her belt, too tight. She likes to look good for her desk. The house is silent. She moves her cup of water to the other side of the dictionary, straightens the stack of sticky notes, colour-orders her pens. And her desk likes to look good for her.

It screams and she feels a fleeting relief, then, in its place, quiet panic. What could it be? Hunger, fear, pain, fear, hunger, pain, fear? They say, *It's just wind, dear.* Such a fierce wind; what the fuck is it doing in there?

She sits at her desk when it sleeps again, staring at someone on the screen.

Second Date

'So,' Louise said and smiled, 'is your degree a BS? Or are you just full of BS?' Her laughter tinkled between them.

He smiled, took a sip of Shiraz. 'It was a *BSc*, actually.'

She rolled her eyes. 'BS, BSc, it's all the same to me.' She flicked open her napkin and draped it across her thighs.

'I'm sure it is,' he said. 'And what was your degree again? A BA did you say? A "Bugger All"?'

She looked up, shocked at the sarcasm.

He went on. 'What did the Arts student say to the Science student after graduation?'

'See ya round?'

'She said, *And would you like fries with that?*' He looked at her, blood behind his cheeks, eyelids lowered, for distance. 'So. Do you have the whole world categorised and reduced or just me? What am I? A character from *Revenge Of The Nerds?*'

'I kind of liked that movie.' A man who blushed had always made her melt.

'I'm no philistine.'

'And I have a real job.'

Tom gulped his wine. She looked away and fiddled with her cutlery.

Her fingertips bouncing on fork tines, she said, 'I thought it was really funny when they set up that camera in the girl's change rooms and the nerds are sitting in their dorm impatiently watching them undress, and finally a girl takes off her underpants and the boys scream, *We have bush!*'

Tom smiled, faintly.

Louise said, 'Come to think of it, these days the line wouldn't be *We have bush*, it would be more like *We have Brazilian!* Don't you think? Or even *We have post-labial-reduction!* Or *We have pre-op-male-to-female!*' She reached for her wine glass, knocked it over into her dinner, her lap, the entire tablecloth. 'Oh God, oh crap, where's the waiter, oh God, oh fuck, I *always* do this.'

He rose with his napkin, crouched in front of her wet dress. 'Here. Let me help.'

Screens 2

Midday soaps, wild crushes, hormones. She is both raw and permeable. Whether Michael will love Jane is of vital importance at this moment. Now, before the commercial break. She *is* Michael and Jane and them together and all of them, all of these characters who stroll through dodgy sets reading bad lines. She is with them all the way. A cry rips her out of the box and tosses her back into the living room. She lifts the child by its armpits and carries it to the change table, her rigid arms stretched straight out. She opens the nappy and, breathing shallowly, she stares, as at a complex yet unpleasant sculpture she is on the brink of understanding. She looks up into its red, unhappy face. She sets to work, two tiny feet pressed together and lifted by one of her hands, holding the bottom aloft. She says, *You know, if you were older, double incontinence would secure you a nursing home bed?* Dodgy sets, bad lines. The unhappy face is undeniably sweet – she can see that – but somehow, it is anonymous. She feels this could be any baby. She looks down at her still–swollen belly. Ha, she thinks, and I told myself I was eating all those pancakes and guzzling all of that maple syrup for *you*. She looks from baby to belly, baby to belly. It had been in there, it had. Encased in a double layer of specially nurtured pale soft pancake. The child's feet are warm in her hand, warm like shells dug out of white sand on some long hot beach. Ipanema, Kauai, St Tropez. All those millions of dead shells warmed in sand and sun, emitting heat like life.

Ingrid

So Ingrid rings her out of the blue. *Sorry it's been so long since I've called. I've been* so busy. And Louise says she'll make them lunch. *Yes*, says Ingrid, *it must be easier for you to stay at home.*

Ingrid: assistant curator at some regional gallery, never progressing in her career as she was (Louise thought) just not that good at curating. They had been friends since university. They strutted round town, shopped, watched movies and ate and drank together until about the time Louise really started to show. Then her pregnancy unmasked something. Ingrid morphed into the beautiful, thin, *sexy* one of the two; she snatched the role and bloomed within it. So that when they shopped, Ingrid would parade around in her still-tiny underwear and tell Louise not to worry, that she knew other women whose bodies didn't change *that* much after birth. *Just some cellulite,* she said, staring at Lou's hips with carefully blanked eyes. Even though it had been Ingrid who – in reality – had the thick waist and the coarse facial features and the short neck and the dry hair. Everyone knew it except Ingrid. (*Don't you think my hair has a celebrity kink to it today?*) Even though it was Ingrid who could never get a date. (*Will Tom be home soon? I want to see what he thinks of my new dress.*) So Louise got fat and pregnant and the world-according-to-Ingrid took precedence; between them it became The World, and bit by bit tiny parts of Louise were crushed, little black ants squashed one by one, leaving unmentionable black smudges of fury – until she'd stopped answering Ingrid's text messages. *Thank God,* Tom said, *I never did like that catty woman.* Then of course he apologised, took her out for dinner, told her repeatedly that she deserved far nicer friends than Ingrid. For months he listened to the endless list of Wrongs Perpetrated Against Her By Ingrid.

Ingrid stood at the threshold in a floral dress that accentuated her thick waist, and she looked Louise up and down, eyes like fat-seeking missiles firing at the pillows above her armpits, the loose lines of her slip.

'Lou! Long time no see!' That fresco smile.

More

She pushes the pram to the café. It's Tuesday. Again. She wades through the heat, sweat dribbling between her thighs, down her legs. She could always not go. But she collects these habits – wading and dragging – until they form currents that carry her. And here she is, wearing dark glasses, rubbing salty water between her ankles, washed up again onto Café Beach. Her child lulled to sleep by the waddle. Everyone orders banana bread and decaf cappuccino. Louise fights the urge to scream, *Just because they call it* bread *doesn't mean it isn't* cake*, you fat fucking cows. It doesn't mean it won't keep your cow-arses fat fat fat.*

She nods periodically, watches deflating milk, peers into the Bugaboo at appropriate intervals. She whispers to the waiter, 'One banana ars . . . I mean bread, please.'

And Then . . .

Tom calling from the front door. *How was your day, honey? . . . Honey? . . . You here? . . . Hon?*

She rolls over, trying to lift her heavy head, trying to get up and out, so Tom doesn't burst in and wake it.

Third Date, In Bed

'So, Tom. Are you by any chance the piper's son?'

'Why, yes, wench, as a matter of fact I am.'

'Why, Tom, that almost makes you an artist!'

'Okay.' He straddles her, pins her arms back into the pillow behind her head. 'Don't say I didn't warn you!'

With Tom

'Once, in third year uni, I was with this lecturer in his office and we were discussing cyberpunk fiction and we started talking about mutant animals and then phosphorescence and then he made a slip-of-the-tongue? Instead of saying, *I could really use a glow-in-the-dark fly*, he said, *I could really use a blow-in-the-dark fly.*'

'Understandable.'

'I couldn't believe it! He didn't even *hear* what he'd said . . . So, what about you?'

'Sure! I'd love one.'

'No! I mean what about you have you ever heard anyone make outrageously revealing slips-of-the-tongue that you can remember?'

'Oh . . . mmm . . . no, not that I've noticed.'

'Well, do you think we should hold someone responsible for their slips-of-the-tongue?'

'Hold someone responsible?'

'Yeah. 'Cause isn't it the case that the slips reveal true feelings?'

'True feelings?'

'Yeah.'

'Aren't they just mistakes?'

'A *blow* in the dark? Come on.'

Tom shrugged. 'I've enough trouble accounting for people's actions.'

'My grandmother always said it was the thought that counted.'

'How traumatising.'

From Ingrid

'You look pretty much the same as you always did. You've just got a bit of a stomach now.'

To Tom

'Can you believe that fucking bitch said I look *pretty much the same as I always did*? Even though I'm *nineteen kilograms* heavier than I used to be? Even though I look like a goddamn cow? I was *never* this fucking fat. I was far better looking than her. She is such a bitch. She thinks she's so fucking gorgeous and someone should tell her to wear foundation over those liverspots, and she actually said she thinks she looks like Angelina Jolie? She pulled a picture she'd cut from a magazine out of her bag to illustrate the resemblance? I mean, that is just psychotic. Oh gosh, I never noticed Angelina's appalling acne scars and lack of a neck before! And you know, she actually asked me when you were due home because she wanted to say hi? As if you would be disappointed if she didn't hang around to say hi? *Hi Tom. Hi Tommy Tom Tom. Wanna feel my smaller arse Tom-Tom? My boobs don't leak. My bra doesn't have wires. I'm a size ten, you know. Oh, you didn't know? Well here, let me rip my top off and show you the fucking* TAG.'

And More

She used to read things other than *The Baby Whisperer, Kid Wrangling, Baby Love, Baby Born.* She used to eat things other than cake. Cake. Cake. Cake. Cake. Cake. Cake. She used to read, ah, who the fuck did she read? Don DeLillo at uni. She remembers that, vaguely. And she must have read Carey, surely, something about a man with no lips in a mouse suit? What has happened to her memory? She worries. Is it prolactin that has her suspended in this fuzzy, fleshy ever-present? Throughout her pregnancy they watched a DVD on the old MacBook almost every night, in bed, their shoulders rubbing, and she can't recall a single plot.

She dresses the baby and sings, *We're goin' to the café and I'm gonna go cra-a-zy, we're goin' to the café and I'm gonna go me-me-mental.*

She dresses herself. Maternity bra. New black cotton underpants. How the fuck, she thinks, can something be full *and* brief? White slip with black trousers. Ballet shoes. A relapse. She just feels false wearing anything else.

At the café, rocking The Ambulator with one foot. *Aha. Aha. Really? Fillet steak for only sixteen ninety-nine? Gosh you're cheap, I mean, that's cheap.* Behind her glasses

Louise crosses her eyes. Shoot me now, no one can see. She holds them that way until the little muscles beside her nose, and the ones inside her temples start to scream. Muscles she didn't know she had, screaming at her. Like childbirth on minimum volume. Like childbirth shushed with a massive morphine OD. It stops her throat from screaming, *Anyone here do with a Blow-In-The-Dark?* Her foot rocks The Ambulator harder, faster. Sunglasses take aim at her ballet slipper. She uncrosses her eyes. She stops rocking.

Who exactly the fuck are these women? These old fucking ugly hags sitting on chairs-de-bistro as if they have massive PVC pipes rammed up their barge arses. Women – *mothers* – discussing all kinds of inane bullshit. What happened to her old friends? What happened to her? Surely this cannot be better than an afternoon in her own home? Louise imagines her desk and then her fridge full of condiments, the drawn curtains, the vomit stain on the living room carpet, Jane and Michael pashing on her TV. She thinks of Ingrid in her size tens and orders the banana bread.

She's next to Pam – who lives five houses down and was probably a perfectly nice and perfectly competent PA in her previous life, exactly the kind of person Louise would never have had to deal with except on the rare occasion that she had to deal with Pam's boss – and Pam discusses all the different kinds, and all the different forms, and all the different colours of the shit that litters her miserable excuse for a life. And Louise shovels banana bread down her throat, imagining all the rotting, black, rancid bananas they must have smashed together to make this cake that smells like a fucking monkey's sweaty arse, and she thinks she might choke.

Home

Eyes closed, it sucks on one breast, and milk flows from both nipples. Her gigantic milk let-down: this engorgement of her breasts feels like a huge inflation, followed by a powerful squeeze. It cries and then – nipple in mouth – it rears back from the fierce rush of milk, gagging. Ever hopeful – in this just like its father – it gives the breast another chance. It drinks easily now, burps, sleeps. Louise lays it in its crib and stands by, making sure it keeps breathing. It does keep breathing, for a long time it keeps breathing. Breathing, and mouthing phantom breasts. And then it cries. Without opening its eyes, it screams for more let-downs. But she leaves it and walks to the toilet. If it's crying it's not dead. She sits. Looks with disgust at her thighs flowing over the edge of the seat and then looks down, at the green tiles and at the empty toilet roll lying like a carcass about 30 cm from the bin.

Right, she says into the empty room. *I mean why would you,* TOM, *put the empty roll in the bin when you can just chuck it on the floor? How idiotic of me not to realise that the* ENTIRE BATHROOM *is your personal rubbish bin. A bin for* ME *to fucking well empty, day after day after day.*

The thought of Tom dropping the empty roll on the floor – brutally, carelessly – is unbearable. She wants to cause him pain. She rips off a handful of paper from the full roll on the holder, wipes herself, stands, viciously pulls up her underwear and, refusing to flush, she goes to feed the kid.

Still More

Louise looks down at her outfit. More uniform than outfit. She looks up and around the table, at the circle of dark glasses. She points to her white slip and says nervously, 'I actually have four of these, you know.' She giggles. She looks from lens to lens. No one responds. They are waiting for the waiter. Louise clears her throat. She is flushing madly and would like to fan her face with the menu. 'Well. You know sweetbreads?' she says, clearly apropos of nothing, voice cracking up. 'I didn't know, but I read that it's an animal's pancreas. But only if you plan to eat it. Because if you're not thinking it's food then it's still called a pancreas. Isn't that weird?'

Pam – feeling obliged as she's sitting right next to Louise – says, 'Hmm, yes.' And then quickly launches into a defence of disposable over cloth. That really gets them going.

Tom

He touches her the way he used to; all of her, as if she's his. There are goose bumps on her skin, a ferocious squeeze inside each breast, then the let-down of her milk. They stop and watch it stream down Tom's chest: thin, white rivulets, the sound of their breathing in the background. The baby starts to cry. Louise whispers, *It can smell me.*

The Page

Bound to her desk again, trying to produce *something* for her sole client. The commission: a web page for a cutting-edge, Asian-fusion women's wear label called High Tea With Mrs Woo. The site has had the word *Brewing* on it for two months now. That single word – tea-coloured and generously surrounded by undulating fleur-de-lis and promiscuous curlicues – is the only thing that separates her from rank housewife. Louise opens her computer and the nausea blooms again, infusing her like a foul tisane. It happens every time: open computer, nausea blooms. She thinks she's Pavlov's dog, the computer her bell, the nausea her saliva. She thinks everything she feels is just habituated reaction.

Brewing. Brewing. Brewing. Luckily, thinks Louise, the High Tea girls are Asian. Patient. Respectful. They knew this project would take time. They understood. Some of their dresses take an experienced seamstress twenty-eight full days to construct. Intricate wearable origami. The garments are phenomenally comfortable. Within them you are as insect in flower, nestling and hidden. Louise flips through look-cards from the current season and wonders again which piece she should buy, if she had money, if it would fit. She narrows it down to two. An orange silk floor-length halter-neck gown or a black wraparound nouveau-kimono jacket. Brewing. Brewing. Brewing. The jacket might hide her gut? She draws a squat Chinese teapot and, in the steam from its spout, imagines a link to the photographs of the collection. The steaming teapot sits on a laden table. There are fortune cookies and bean cakes and tiny teacups with koi. And then she is cut with the frenzied, rasping scream of a baby being tortured in its flannelette swaddle, abandoned, dying. Louise gently closes the computer. Milk. Milk. Milk. One litre of milk is enough for forty cups of tea, or one hungry baby. She pushes her palms together.

Dough

'Honey! I'm home! I bought you that breadmaker you've been wanting for ages!'

Louise walks to the front door, frowning. 'That *what* I've been wanting?'

'The breadmaker! I researched them and I've bought the super deluxe model that bips so you can add sultanas and nuts, or herbs, or whatever you want mid-cycle? So they don't get crushed by the kneading?'

'What are you talking about?'

'The breadmaker! You said they were great and you had to get one, when we went to that kid's ridiculous one-month-old birthday party that time? Remember?'

Louise turns and walks back to the kitchen.

'Louise?'

'The dinner's burning.'

'But I thought you wanted one.'

'Tom,' she says and spins around blinking at him like she's trying to clear oil from her eyes, 'I was lying?'

All This Came From Their One Little Slip

It is tiny and blind and squints when it looks up at her. Squints through opaque blue eyes that are always searching for her, waiting for her. And Tom's body is so hard and always ready, always waiting for her, too. Muscular, masculine, gorgeous, terrifying in its ready waiting. And Louise's body – she peeks down at the flabby contours as she steps out of the shower – is this white dough, risen and soft and waiting also, waiting to be punched down or something. And it seems to her that she is separate from all of them that make up this nice little family.

Among Surgeons, A Fat Gut Is Called An Apron

Jewel from High Tea With Mrs Woo calls. Louise imagines Jewel holding her iPhone against the shiny hair that bobs above her origami clothes. Black on black on black. Luckily Louise has changed, and is sitting at her desk in ballet slippers and red lipstick, so she can pose with fingers draped over her forehead, other hand cradling her Bakelite phone. *Sure, sure. The cascading style sheets are the struggle.* She is sweating. *Yeah, look. It's almost there. I should have the mock-up to you by Friday latest.* The tone is important. There's only High Tea between herself and obliteration. Only this single-thread-page. She shakes her hair like a wet dog, trying to clear the fog, and looks down at what she has. Sepia-toned curlicues are not very Asian, but still. She closes her eyes and pushes hard against her eyelids. She once read this could make you faint. She is, in truth, so tired she could splinter, and fainting sounds like bliss. She walks to the bedroom and stands in front of the wardrobe mirror just to check there's something that sort-of-looks-pretty-much-like-her-with-a-stomach really there. *Motherfucker.* She steps closer. She barely fits inside. Breath from her hot lips fogs the mirror and her face disappears.

Check-Up

Louise straps the baby's bassinet into the car and drives to her doctor. She's cancelled the appointment three times and is too embarrassed not to turn up. Although she does not need a doctor. What she needs is a new body and a new wardrobe. A new car would be nice – a two-seater convertible. Tom's okay for now, as is the house, but everything else she needs renewed. A doctor cannot help her with this. She skulks inside the surgery, hands her Medicare card to the receptionist, places the bassinet on the floor, baby lulled to sleep by the drive, and takes a seat. She has the first appointment after lunch and is the only patient waiting. She looks at the clock on the pastel blue wall. What does a doctor eat for lunch? Probably lettuce. Mesclun. Radicchio. Mache. Dr Taylor, mid-forties, looking like every other female

GP Louise has ever known – sort of mouse-brown and *inoffensive* – calls her in. Louise hauls the bassinet into the room and sets it down again with a sigh. The child is still asleep.

'So,' says Dr Taylor, hands on her knees, and then smiles in that way they do.

Louise raises her eyebrows and tries to smile back.

'How old is the little one now?'

'Three months.'

'And how's it all going?'

'Oh, it's fine.' Dr Taylor has a large, bright red tomato sauce stain on her cream cardigan, just above her right breast. Louise can't help but stare.

The doctor looks down, touches the sauce stain. 'I shouldn't wear cream, I do this *every* time. I'm absolutely hopeless.'

And suddenly Louise is crying. 'I'm sorry,' she sobs into her palms, 'I never do this, I never cry in public. I don't know what's got into me, I'm fine, really.'

'You never cry in public? God, you should try it, gets you great seats on the train.'

Louise smiles faintly, tears trek down her cheeks. 'I'm just so tired . . . and . . . so bored . . . I could start peeling my skin for entertainment. What's wrong with me? Isn't this supposed to be heaven on earth?'

'Yes. Well. I don't know about that. But. Well. Are you sleeping?'

Louise shakes her head. 'Barely.'

'How's your appetite?'

Louise snorts and smacks at a thigh.

'Intimate relations?'

Louise blinks at the ceiling. 'The milk.' She waves her hand in front of her breasts. 'And,' she says, waving her hand over her lap, lowering her voice, 'it's dryish.'

'Topical oestrogen will help with that. I'll give you a script. But, Louise, do you imagine hurting yourself?'

Louise shakes her head. 'I'm not going to kill myself. I'm just . . . unhappy.'

'You know, some mothers adore this very-young-baby stage. They love the helplessness, or dependence maybe. Or they find every little event – wee, poo, burp, fart, the lot – fascinating. And then there are mothers who only start to enjoy themselves when the kid starts to talk . . . That was definitely me, I can tell you.'

'Really?'

'*Hated* the first twelve months, every time. Adore them beyond belief now they're in school.'

Louise smiles and closes her eyes. She opens them. 'Can I have some diet pills?'

Dr Taylor laughs.

Tuesday

The cries, and cries, and the cries. She picks it up and it blinks long, wet eyelashes. The lips are pink and smell like sweetest milk. She brushes them against her cheek. The baby is happy to let her do it. It is happy just to feel her. All it wants is her skin and her milk. It's Tuesday, but she cannot face all those struggling-to-be-brave faces. She stays at home in a crisp, clean white slip, without trousers. Barefoot and barefaced she feels her soft thighs rub against each other and, for the first time, it does not repulse her. It feels only soft. Soft and baby powder dry. She potters in the kitchen, her baby in a sling. She makes a tomato sandwich, throws chicken, onions and wine into a cast-iron pot, reads the breadmaker instruction booklet. In the afternoon she lies on the bed with the baby on her chest. She hums an old song. *We'll start at the very beginning, a very good place to start* . . . She lets it gorge, watches the eyes blink their magnificent lashes, lips against her skin.

'Hey, baby, if you tell me I'm beautiful I'll give you milk till you're ten.' Baby eyes open and look up. 'There's a good girl.'

She wakes to the sound of Tom opening the front door, the baby asleep in the crook of her arm. Tom drops his bag in the hallway and calls out, 'Lou? Lou-Lou? . . . Mmm! Fresh bread!'

I have always imagined that paradise will be a kind of library.

— *Jorge Luis Borges*

Acknowledgements

I thank Lyn Tranter of Australian Literary Management and Rod Morrison of Picador for noticing me, picking me up and setting me down safely on a shelf.

I thank Jo Jarrah for her sharp eye for inconsistency, contradiction and plain old stuff-ups; Anna Valdinger for her enthusiasm and her gently-put dissatisfactions which were always enlightening and inspiring. I was grateful to receive constructive, intelligent feedback from Kirsten Tranter, and from the students and staff of the School of English, University of Newcastle.

I have had the privilege to be befriended, heard and read by some of the most talented readers and writers in the country. I thank Judith Beveridge for her poet's eye and intricate reading, for her encouragement and fierce belief in my work. It had such a force it threw me out of my front door; big yellow envelope addressed to Lyn Tranter in my hand. I thank Helen Garner for a friendship that gives me immense happiness, hilarity and food for thought, and for her generous offers to read and re-read the earliest of drafts. I thank Oscar Zentner – careful listener and legendary reader – for his uncompromising benevolence.

For their friendship, patience, support and tutelage I offer my immense gratitude to a group of the most intelligent and inspiring people I have ever known: Dr Kirsten Murray, Dr Krishnan Gupta, Dr Trevor Mallard, Prof Jonathan Silberberg, Dr John Olsen, and all of their marvellous families. Without you I would have run from the hospital – tearing at my hair, wild-eyed and screaming – and burnt the path behind me so that I could never follow it back inside by accident.

For offering me a calm, flexible space to practise medicine (with ambient lighting, endless morning teas and triathlon-training-tips on tap), I thank the Department of Nuclear Medicine, John Hunter Hospital.

I thank Dr Mitchell Lawlor: dearest friend, valued reader and photographer-in-chief.

And most of all I offer love and gratitude to my magnificent family – my greatest supporters, my inspiration and joy: the late Yvonne Burnside (Nan), the late Barry Hitchcock (Dad), Jillian Hitchcock (Mum), Robert and Kathy-Lee Hitchcock, Jennie and Shane McKenzie, and a million billion trillion times over – Michael, Ida and Yve.

The following stories have appeared in slightly or substantially different versions in the following places:

'Poetics of Space': *The Sleepers Almanac* No. 3, Sleepers Publishing, 2007; *The Best Australian Stories 2008*, Edited by Delia Falconer, Black Inc., 2008

'Blood': *The Sleepers Almanac* No. 4, Sleepers Publishing, 2008; *Families: Modern Australian Stories* Volume VI, Edited by Barry Oakley, The Five Mile Press, 2008

'Some Kind of Fruit': *The Best Australian Stories 2007*, Edited by Robert Drewe, Black Inc., 2007

'Tactics': *Griffith Review* 13, Griffith University/ABC Books, 2006; *The Best Australian Stories 2006*, Edited by Robert Drewe, Black Inc., 2006; ABC Radio National Short Story Program 2008

'Weightlessness': *The Sleepers Almanac* No. 3, Sleepers Publishing, 2007

'In Formation': *Meanjin* Vol. 63 No. 4, 2004; *Psychotherapy In Australia* Vol 12 No 1, Psychoz Publications, 2005

Debra Adelaide
The Household Guide to Dying

When Delia Bennet – author and domestic advice column-
ist – is diagnosed with cancer, she knows it's time to get
her house in order. After all, she's got to secure the future
for her husband, their two daughters and their five beloved
chickens. But as she writes lists and makes plans, questions
both large and small creep in. Should she divulge her best
culinary secrets? Read her favourite novels one last time?
Plan her daughters' far-off weddings?

Complicating her dilemma is the matter of the past, and a
remote country town where she fled as a pregnant teenager,
only to leave broken-hearted eight years later.

Researching and writing her final *Household Guide*, Delia is
forced to confront the pieces of herself she left behind. She
learns what matters is not the past but the present – that
the art of dying is all about truly living.

Fresh, witty, deeply moving – and a celebration of love,
family and that place we call home – this unforgettable story
will surprise and delight the reader until the very last page.

Judith Lanigan
A True History of the Hula Hoop

A beguiling and utterly original debut novel about two women born centuries apart but joined by the spirit of adventure and a quest for true love.

Catherine is a hula-hooping performance artist, a talented and independent individual plying her trade on the international burlesque stage. Each year she tours the European festival circuit, delighting her audiences and honing her skills. But behind the glittering and bohemian façade, Catherine knows that security is hard won and that true love is elusive. As she nears the middle of her life – admired but impoverished – she begins to question the nature of her vocation and the sacrifices women must make in order to succeed.

Columbina, meanwhile, is a feisty female clown and a principal in a 16th-century Italian *commedia dell'arte* troupe. Commissioned to perform for the King of France, the troupe makes its way across a Europe held back by centuries of inequality and rocked by religious wars. As they near the city of Lyon, they are attacked by hooligans, only to be rescued by a group of marauding Huguenots with their own agenda . . . Using all their ingenuity, the troupe must hatch a daring escape plan if they have any hope of survival, let alone reaching France.

As Catherine and Columbina struggle to make sense of an increasingly nonsensical world – and to assert their rights as performers and women during times of profound change – their lives, as if by magic, seem to interact. The result is an inspiring, surprising tale about following your dreams, staying true to your heart and always believing in magic.

Alison Wong
As the Earth Turns Silver

It is 1905 and brothers Yung and Shun eke out a living as green grocers in Wellington's bustling Chinatown. Recently-arrived immigrants, the pair must support their families back home in China, but know they must adapt if they are to survive and prosper in their adopted home.

On the other side of town, Katherine McKechnie struggles to raise her rebellious son and daughter following the death of her husband Donald. A strident right-wing newspaper-man, Donald terrorised his family, though was idolised by his teenage son.

On her way home from work one day, Katherine chances upon Yung's grocery store and is touched by the Chinaman's unexpected generosity. Soon a clandestine relationship develops between the immigrant and the widow, a relation-ship Katherine's son Robbie cannot abide . . .

On the eve of World War I, as young men are swept up on a tide of macho patriotism, Robbie takes his family's honour into his own hands. In doing so, he places his mother at the heart of a tragedy that will affect everyone and everything she holds dear.

Powerful, moving and utterly unforgettable, *As the Earth Turns Silver* announces the arrival of a bold new voice in contemporary fiction.

Philip Hui
Superbia

su•per•bi•a (su-ˈpər-bē-ə) | noun
1 pride; an inordinately high opinion of oneself; an excessive aspiration to excellence
2 the deadliest of the seven deadly sins; the sin from which all other sins arise

ORIGIN: Latin, *superbus* 'proud, haughty, arrogant'

Jason Roche, an Australian working in London's foreign exchange, believes a life is only well lived if you're the centre of a glittering universe – big bucks in the bank, a swank flat in Belgravia, an Aston Martin in the garage and a trophy fiancée in the bedroom. This is London, 2003, awash with money, sex, drugs and all the bling filthy lucre can buy . . .

Enter Zach, Jason's eccentric brother-in-law-to-be, who has come home to put his affairs in order, before returning to Japan to take his vows with a sect of Buddhist zealots.

Determined to bring Zach to his senses, Jason sets out to lure him back to the worldly ways of the upper-class existence he left behind. But as Jason's precarious reality starts to crack, he must confront the possibility that it just might be he who is in need of salvation – from the person he has become.

A stunning literary debut set in a society in the grip of the last days of decadence, *Superbia* is a fast-paced, fun-park ride through the seven deadly sins, and their roots in our obsession with love and sex, class and power, youth and celebrity, and the enduring tension between materiality and spirituality.

Michael McGirr
The Lost Art of Sleep

A wise and funny exploration of quite possibly the best third of your life by the acclaimed author of *Things You Get For Free* and *Bypass*.

Bed is the most dangerous place on earth. More people die there than anywhere else. Maybe that's why each passing generation spends less time in bed than the one before.

The arrival of baby twins sent Michael McGirr in search of an ancient practice for which bed is the ideal setting. It's called sleep.

In this warm, witty and engaging book, McGirr muses on the many benefits of sleep; mourns its demise; explains aspects of its strange personality; observes what the brain really gets up to in the small hours; and makes acquaintance with some of the great sleepers and wakers of history, from Aristotle to Thomas Edison, from Homer to Florence Nightingale, from Shakespeare to Peter Pan.

Both a personal journey and a profound exploration of one of life's true constants, *The Lost Art of Sleep* proves that there are few situations which can't be helped by a good night's kip.

Emily Maguire
Smoke in the Room

The searing new novel from the internationally-acclaimed author of *Taming the Beast, The Gospel According to Luke* and *Princesses & Pornstars.*

Nights were okay if she distracted herself with what CDs she wanted or how to find the money for more grog. With sex and shops and food and TV commercials. With a sad man and his corny tattoos. The stuff of life was all distraction, and distraction allowed her to get on with the stuff of life. But nobody stays distracted. The song ends and the man sleeps and the alcohol wears off and there it is; the window, the truck, the bread knife in its stay-sharp sheath.

Katie Lewis is a little screwed up. She can't help complicating things – in particular, relationships. But when Adam, the displaced American, and Graeme, the weary martyr, land on her doorstep, salvation may be at hand.

Over one sultry summer, this unlikely cast of three will wrestle with some of life's most poignant questions: how to live, how to love, and how to stay cool when all around you burns . . .

Provocative, honest, brimming with sexual tension and crackling with intelligence, Emily Maguire's sensational new novel cements her place as one of Australia's hottest young talents.